FICTION

CAPES AND MASKS
Richard Helms 2

THE WILL AND WAYNE SHOW
Adam Chase 16

MURDERER'S PARADISE
Michael Mallory 25

THE ILLUSION OF CONTROL
Josh Pachter 44

SPEAK OF THE DEVIL
Jeanne DuBois 47

THE IMPATIENT INMATE
Michael Scherer 60

REMOTE STORAGE
Susan Hammerman 69

DINNER AND ...
Bruce Harris 78

FACE THE MUSIC
A You-Solve-It By Peter DiChellis 86

INQUIRIES & ADVERTISING

Address: Suite 22, 509 Commissioners Road West, London, Ontario, N6J 1Y5
Advertising: Email info@mysteryweekly.com
Editor: Kerry Carter **Publisher:** Chuck Carter **Cover Artist:** Robin Grenville Evans
Submissions: https://mysteryweekly.com/submit.asp
Mystery Weekly Magazine is published monthly by AM Marketing Strategies.

CAPES AND MASKS

Richard Helms

"You know the story. Stolen by aliens who crashed my fourth birthday party. Returned when I was seventeen, but I was somehow ... *different* than when I left. Well, *duh*. I was thirteen years older, had all this weird hair growing where it never had, and my voice sounded like I was shaving a cat with a cheese grater. Had never seen a human girl naked, but by gods I wanted to for some reason. Hey, you try spending your entire childhood with cold-blooded amphibians from the planet Flax and see if you don't return a little bent. I still can't eat fish.

"Of course, there were ... *other* differences. My foster parents, Koxm and Borquash, allowed the Flaxigians to experiment with my DNA. They tweaked and modified, and before I knew it, I was able to do all this *stuff*.

"Like the flying thing. What's up with that? I don't have wings. I weigh two hundred pounds, and yet I only *think* about flying and I'm levitating two feet off the ground. It can get really unnerving. I don't care how long I've done it, I'm still queasy hovering ten thousand feet over the city, waiting for someone to do something illegal. I mean, if I suddenly lose the powers, I'm coming down like a cannonball, and I'm screaming like a little girl all the way. Bet that would make some headlines.

"Then there's the strength. I can bench press an ocean liner. What good is a power like that? You can only hit a guy so hard before you inflict the kind of injuries that land you in court. The police have tried to register me as a weapon of mass destruction. Sometimes, you can be too strong. Like the time I was late for a date, and I pulled the door of the cab into the back seat with me when I slammed it.

"And the bullet thing. Yeah, they bounce off my chest. Let me tell you, though, it really *hurts*. I have nerve endings. The prisons are full of guys walking around bragging about how they bounced .45 caliber slugs off my nipples. Meanwhile, I can't get out of bed the next day.

"Sometimes I wish I was like Stealth. All he does is skulk around looking like a reject from the Boise Light Opera production of *Cats*, waiting for criminals to strike. He doesn't have any powers. He can't fly, or see through concrete walls, or hear a flea scratching its butt in the Yukon. He's just cool. And he can fight really well. He had the right idea. He trained for almost ten years to get into the hero game.

"Me, I got dropped out of a spaceship over Nebraska with scrambled chromosomes and a couple of videodisks containing instructions on how to use my powers only for good. Hell, man, I was seventeen years old. I didn't give a damn at that age about fighting crime. Even if I did, can you imagine how embarrassing it would be if I got a woody in the tights? Kids that age get a diamond cutter if you look at them sideways. I can hear it now. *Hey, Captain Courage, what's with the pup tent?*

"That's another thing. Everyone presumes I came up with that name. Man, if I meant to become a superhero, do you think I'd have dug up a lame-o handle like *Captain Courage*? Some reporter came up with it. After the newspaper printed the name Captain Courage a couple of days running, I was pretty much stuck with it.

"Then there's the issue of money. You'd think, after I saved New York City from imminent destruction a couple of times, they'd put me on the payroll. But *nooooo*. They give me this big cheesy plywood key covered in gold foil." I balled my fist and laid it over my heart. "Sometimes, it just gets me, right *here*, you know?"

I took another healthy chug from the flagon of Budweiser.

"Bitch, bitch, bitch," Blade Mistress said, from the bar stool next to mine. "It's always the same rant with you, Cap. Life is what it is. Live with the cards you've been dealt. Bloom where you're planted."

I sneaked a super-quick glance at her cleavage, pushed up like fleshy basketballs from the gold piping of the multicolored bustier she used as her costume. She was seven feet of icy blonde superbabe. I'd have given anything for X-ray vision. Why'd the comic book guys get all the coolest powers?

I gestured toward her beer.

"How about another?" I said.

"No thanks. I'm flying. Hey, did you hear about Sunburst?"

"What about him?"

"He's dead."

I had my beer halfway to my mouth, but I stopped and set it back down on the counter.

"Harvey's dead? How'd it happen?"

"Who knows? His landlady smelled this rancid odor coming from his apartment. She called the cops. They found him lying on the couch, staring at the ceiling. I heard he'd been dead about three days."

"Wonder how he died. I'm betting on a stroke. Harvey was always wound way too tight."

"Here's the funny thing, though," Blade Mistress said, as she drew circles in the pool of condensation from her mug on the bar. "He was wearing the costume."

"The Sunburst getup?"

"Yeah. Like he put it on to go out on patrol, and then just died on the couch."

"Who told you?"

"Oh, those guys. You know. The new ones. They wear solid black scaly Kevlar and ski goggles."

"Can't place them. What kind of powers do they have?"

"Damned if I know. From what I can tell, they kill with their breath. Hey, you oughta look into the Sunburst thing. You know, *not* as Captain Courage."

I knew. Like just about every guy who battled crime in tights, I had a secret identity. Blade Mistress didn't need one. She had a secret hideout way beneath the city, and an independent income from her grandmother, who was some kind of goddess or something on her planet. Some people get all the luck.

Me, I had to make a living on top of saving the world. When the Flaxigians dropped me out of their spaceship into the cornfield, they neglected to leave behind a ton of gold or some precious diamonds I could salt away to buy myself some cool digs and pay for my food and dry cleaning and stuff. I needed a day job.

As it turned out, four capes already worked at the local newspaper. No imagination.

My friend Jesse—you know him as Vulturo—owns a bookstore but pays a bunch of kids minimum wage to run it so he can duck out any time his arch-enemy, Doctor Crunch, busts out of prison.

The Velvet Spike still lives with his mother. I mean, sure, she was Queen Chaos back in the day, but now she's just his mom, and Spikey lives in her basement.

Me? I took the only thing I could find where I was certain not to have any competition. I became Eddie Shane, Private Eye.

No conflict of interest there. I do strictly domestic work. Let Eamon Gold and Magnum and Spenser deal with all the mob bosses and psychopaths. I prefer to spend my time sitting outside a seedy motel, waiting for some dentist to finish boinking his secretary so I can take his picture as he walks her to the car. Lemme tell you, Sparky, there is no better source of cashflow than spurned housewives. Also, they love revenge sex. Man, if only they knew when they were in bed with Eddie Shane that they were actually squirming all over Captain Courage. They'd totally plotz.

"I don't do that kind of work," I said.

“Yeah, I know. Divorce surveillance only. You have a license though. You could investigate Sunburst’s murder if you wanted to.”

“We got police for that.”

“What in hell kind of superhero are you, anyway?” she said, her voice thick and slurred.

“If you’re so interested, why don’t *you* check it out?”

“Can’t,” she said. Then she hiccupped. “Vicki and I are going on vacation. Taking a trip to Cabo. Swift is covering my calls until I get back.”

“Vacation sounds good,” I said, and grabbed the bartender’s attention.

I had the flu a couple of years back. Laid me flat on my back in bed for a week. The newspapers went ballistic, wondering where Captain Courage had gone. It was gratifying, in a way, but sometimes this city can be *so* needy.

Since then, I make a point of flying around at least once a day, preferably buzzing a rooftop party or a Yankees’ game, so there are lots of witnesses.

I pounded back another couple of beers, which for me was like drinking water since my metabolism works at the speed of light. Then I flew around the city once or twice just to put in an appearance.

After a couple of tours around town, I took a quick dash through the park and flew straight to my apartment in Weehawken. Even Captain Courage can’t afford to live in Manhattan. Most of the capes and masks live in the outer boroughs or in Jersey. We even keep our favorite hangout, Sam’s Heroes Bar, in Hoboken.

I stowed my costume in the false back of my closet and changed into a tee shirt and a pair of cutoffs. I had DVR’d *The Voice* and *The Bachelor* while I was at the bar. I wasn’t nearly sleepy enough to hit the rack, so I turned on the television.

The screen had a wide banner at the bottom, with the words *Special Report* trailing across it, and showed what looked like an excavated hole in the ground, ringed with flames. I thumbed the volume control.

“... Just in the last five minutes, Taffy. Neighbors reported the sound of a jet plane, but nobody saw the impact.”

I had a sick feeling in my stomach, and it wasn’t the street cart halal I’d scarfed down for dinner. A jet plane crashing in the middle of Coney Island with no witnesses and no debris could only mean one thing.

I grabbed my phone and dialed Blade Mistress’s cell. It rang, and rang, and rang, until finally her voicemail kicked in. I clicked off the phone without leaving a message. She wouldn’t get it anyway.

It took twenty seconds to fly to Coney Island on afterburner. I didn't want to drop in as Captain Courage, at least not yet. Instead, I changed into my Eddie Shane duds behind an air conditioning unit and made my way around to the flashing lights.

A uniformed cop approached me as I neared the scattered flames, which still flickered in the smoky night. He held up a hand.

"Sorry, sir, this is a restricted area."

"Hold up, there," someone said.

I looked over the cop's shoulder, and saw Tom Holden, a fifteen-year gold shield with the NYPD, Coney Island Division.

"Eddie Shane, PI," he said, as he shouldered past the cop. "Long time, no see. I thought we punched your ticket on the Big Enchilada Extortion Case."

"I solved that one for you. Dirty Sanchez and his henchmen will spend the next forty years in orange jumpsuits, thanks to me."

I held up a palm, and he took a couple of speed bag punches at it. It was very macho and collegial. Tom and I have known each other for years. He only knows me as Eddie Shane. He doesn't have a clue I'm also the other guy.

"So, what do you know?" I asked, nodding toward the fires.

"Something augured in about a half hour ago. Dug a hole and caught the local flora on fire. We can't find much debris. Some of the guys think it was a bomb."

"Or maybe ... an invisible jet plane?" I suggested.

"An invisible jet plane ..." Holden said, chuckling. "That's rich. ... Hold on. An invisible jet plane. Yeah. You know what that means, don't you?"

I nodded and opened my notepad.

"Thought you'd like to know that Blade Mistress was in the air tonight. She and Vicki Valiant were flying to Cabo for ... uh, for a mercy mission." I tactfully danced around their real reason for the trip. It wasn't necessary, at least yet, for *everyone* to know their business.

"Vicki Valiant, Intrepid Girl Reporter?" Tom asked. He let out a low whistle. "You think ..."

He pointed toward the smoking hole in the ground.

"Yeah, Tom. I think," I said. "That's not all. I heard earlier this evening that Sunburst bought it."

"Yeah."

"Doesn't that sound suspicious to you?"

"How so?"

"Two masks and a famous crusading heroine reporter taking the dirt nap in only three days? I don't like coincidences."

Tom stroked his chin and narrowed his eyes.

"It's suspicious at that, ain't it?" he said.

We were interrupted by the squeal of tortured rubber, as an obsidian armored car careened around the corner, broke traction, did two quick three-sixties, and came to rest five feet from us. Twin gull-wing doors popped open. Stealth, his bulletproof calico body armor gleaming, sprung out, followed closely by his plucky boy sidekick, Felix.

"You're too late," Tom said as they stepped up to us. "Eddie Shane PI here already figured out that the plane ..."

"... Belonged to Blade Mistress," Stealth finished. The electrical transducers in his cowl transformed his voice into a purring approximation of a cat's meow. "Yes. We know. Felix and I came as soon as we saw the Stealth Signal."

I looked up at the sky. There were a few wispy clouds, but it was otherwise empty.

"What signal?" I said. "I don't see anything."

"Well, duh!" Felix said. "It's a *Stealth* Signal, Shane."

Stealth tapped his cowl.

"Special filters. Only Felix and I can see the signal."

One of the officers combing the crash site straightened up and waved his arms. "I got something, Detective!"

"You wait here," Tom told us, and ran toward the officer.

"What's the matter?" Felix chortled. "Why did you come as the B Team, Shane? Captain Courage got a date with his fist tonight?"

Stealth reached out and rubbed my jacket lapel between his thumb and forefinger.

"What's with the trench coat and the slouch fedora, Eddie? It's, like, August."

"Yeah," Felix said, "And it's also, like, the twenty-first century."

"You let your sidekick talk too much," I told Stealth.

"Tough words for a guy who was raised by sushi," Felix shot back.

"That's enough, little chum," Stealth said.

"How did you guys know this was Blade Mistress's jet?" I asked.

"Simple deductive logic," Stealth mewed. "Blade Mistress's underground lair is right next to The Sensational Shrew's network of burrows, roughly a hundred feet below the foundation of the Empire State Building. Her invisible jet launch pad runs at an angle of fourteen degrees across the east side of Midtown, exiting just under the Roosevelt Expressway. Climbing at a rate of approximately one thousand feet per minute, at a speed of three hundred miles per hour, and accounting for the dip she had to make under the Brooklyn Bridge, I deduced she would have reached a height of just under seven thousand feet when her jet nosed over. Given the mass of the jet, I can see by the depth of the hole it left that it hit the ground at a little over five hundred miles per hour. I ran all the data through the StealthPuter in the Stealth Catbox, which pinpointed the probable origin point of the jet, and the conclusion was—as they say—foregone."

"How about you?" Felix asked. "How'd *you* figure it out, Cap?"

"Hey, kid. Call me *Eddie* when I'm wearing the fedora. Blade Mistress and I tossed back a couple at the Heroes Bar earlier this evening. She told me she and Vicki Valiant were flying to Cabo tonight for a week of margaritas and carpet munching. That and, of course, the *jet plane was INVISIBLE*!"

I shouted the last word, to make my point. There was, after all, only one invisible jet in the world. Even a mentally deficient degenerate toady like Felix should have been able to figure that one out.

"Yes," Stealth said. "I suppose that would be another way. I, uh, guess you've already made the connection between this crash and what happened to Harvey?"

"Tom and I were talking about it just before you showed up."

"A strange business," he said. "It's almost as if someone were trying to take out the masks one by one."

"Your computer tell you that one too?"

"No. Just finely tuned feline intuition."

"Give it a break, Myron," I said, being careful say his secret identity name quietly. "You aren't a cat. You're a human being in a cat suit with an electronic voicebox."

"But, with the grace, instincts, and intelligence of a cat," he argued.

"I have a hard time believing any significant crime fighting is likely to be done by an animal that spends three quarters of the day asleep and the other quarter licking its butt. I gotta go. Blade Mistress's partner is probably a wreck. I need to comfort her. You guys hang around here, see if Tom finds anything useful."

Blade Mistress's partner was a nice kid named Alexandra Pitsikoulis, but everyone knew her as Zandy. She was a year out of high school and lived in a rent-controlled studio apartment in SoHo that she had inherited from her grandmother. Her cape name was Swift because she was—well—really really fast.

She opened the door an instant before I knocked on it.

Like I said, she's really really fast.

She already had the local news on the television when I arrived. She stood in front of the set, gnawing at one knuckle. Her eyes were red, and her cheeks were tear-streaked. She launched herself at my chest and hung on tight.

"I just came from the crash site," I told her. "I'm sorry to be the one to tell you, but it's almost certainly Blade Mistress's jet. Not only that, but she told me earlier this evening that she was taking Vicki Valiant with her to Mexico."

"Oh, Eddie!" she sobbed. "What happened? How could she have just ... *crashed* like that?"

"That's what I'm trying to find out, Sugarcheeks," I said. "Let's sit down."

She calmed down after a couple of minutes.

"This is just terrible."

"I know. I promise you, Zandy, I'll find out who did it. Blade Mistress told me about Sunburst at the bar tonight," I said. "She suggested I might want to look into it. You know, as Eddie Shane."

Her eyes grew wide.

"You think Harvey might have been screwing someone's wife?" she asked.

I sighed. You do enough divorce work, and people think it's *all* you can do.

"Not like that," I said. "She thought Harvey might have been murdered."

"Oooohhhhh," she said.

I mentioned that Zandy is really really fast. I didn't say she was bright. That's why she was a sidekick.

"Did Blade Mistress discuss Harvey with you?" I asked.

"No. Why? Do you think she might have had some idea who killed him?"

"She was a great pilot, kid. She could fly that plane through the arch at Columbus Circle without scuffing the paint, or whatever it was coated with. I can't believe she'd just auger in like that unless the jet was sabotaged."

"And that would mean she was murdered!" Swift said.

"Which is what she thought happened to Sunburst. So, we have two masks killed in one week. And you know what that means, don't you?"

"What?" she asked.

I pronounced, solemnly, "Bad things always come in threes."

I was halfway back to my apartment when I remembered something Blade Mistress had said during my self-indulgent whine session earlier in the evening. The two new masks had told her about Sunburst dying. She had implied they hung out at the bar. Maybe they were legit and knew something that could help.

I banked toward the river as I passed over the Empire State Building, taking time to shoot a quick wave at the tourists on the observation deck. Doesn't cost me a thing, and it's great PR. I arrived at the bar in Hoboken half a minute later, changed back into Eddie's clothes, and walked in.

Sam, the guy who runs the place, grabbed my arm as soon as I crossed the doorway.

"Sorry, Eddie," he said, pointing to a sign over the bar. "No cape, no mask, no service."

"It's me," I said. "Cap."

"I know, but rules is rules. You gotta put the suit on."

"Aw, c'mon, Sam. I just got out of it. You have any idea how hard it is to put on the suit, take it off, and put it back on again? The Flaxigians might have invented Spandex before they discovered fire, but they never got around to the zipper. If I stretch out the neck hole too much, my cape just isn't going to hang right. We don't want that, do we? Nobody likes a sloppy superhero."

"I feel for ya, dude. I really do. I don't make the rules. Either put the suit back on, or you know what."

I winced. *'You know what'* was no fun. On the other hand, I'd already gotten the damned thing sweaty. Climbing into a damp costume is no fun either.

"Just give it to me," I said, scowling.

Sam handed me a cape about twice the size of a lobster bib. It was pink and tied around my neck with a shoestring. On the back was a picture of a sparkly unicorn prancing on top of a rainbow.

It was the Cape of Shame.

It didn't go with the trench coat at all.

"Okay," I said, as I finished tying it. "I got some bad news, bro. It looks like Blade Mistress crashed her jet in Brooklyn tonight."

"She was just here a couple of hours ago!" Sam said, tearing up. "What happened?"

"The hot money is on sabotage. You know Sunburst died, right?"

"Sure. Harvey was a walking landmine. I was surprised he didn't stroke out years ago."

"Yeah, but get this. According to Blade Mistress, he was wearing his rig when he died. Laid out on the couch in full costume, like he was in a coffin or something. From what Blade Mistress told me, it sounds like he was posed."

"Who would do that?"

"Someone who liked him a lot, or maybe someone sending a message. Blade Mistress said she learned about Harvey from a couple of new masks. She didn't know their names."

"You mean the guys all in black with the bug-eye goggles?"

"Yeah. That's how she described them. I haven't seen them yet. Are they here?"

"Naw. They were around earlier this evening. The tall one goes by Goldfinch. The little one calls himself Scarlet Wasp. Can't figure out the black costumes. Ain't a bit of gold or red on them. Rookies. Go figure."

"You know anything about them? Where they live?"

"Nope. They just showed up a couple of weeks ago. Goldfinch says they moved here from Peoria. They did some vigilante work out there. Wanted to break into the big time."

"City's getting swarmed with capes and masks. Just about every neighborhood has their own superhero. They got four of them rumbling around Hell's Kitchen. SoHo's lousy with them, and don't get me started on Midtown. We have so many here, they're overflowing onto Long Island. You think, maybe, these new guys might want to carve out a niche they can fit into? Create an opening by taking out a few of the established guys?"

"Like Harvey?"

"He'd be a great place to start. Wouldn't look suspicious if a tightly wound guy like Harvey pulled the pin. Once the police finish their investigation, I bet they'll peg Blade Mistress's crash as an accident. Boom. Two openings in less than a week, and no clear evidence of a crime. Since this Goldfinch character and his sidekick—what in hell does he call himself again?"

"Scarlet Wasp."

"Yeah. Him. Since they both seemed to know about Harvey before anyone else, it would be interesting to find out what else they know. I'm gonna work the room. See if anyone else here knows anything about them."

Two beers and a couple of trips around the bar yielded nothing. I thought about planting myself in the corner with a pitcher, wait around a bit, maybe see if they showed up, but then I thought better of it. I'm super. I could get to the bar from my apartment in about five seconds on afterburner. Sam had to be at the bar. I didn't. I asked him to call me if the noobs showed their faces, and I headed home.

My phone rang two hours later. It was Sam.

"Those two guys showed up. Only hung around for a coupla minutes. They said they had to meet a guy at Pier 86," Sam said.

"That's where the *USS Intrepid* is moored. The aircraft carrier. What business could they have there?"

"Beats me. They were in a hurry though."

I had tossed the Captain Courage costume into the drier as soon as I got home. It was still toasty warm as I pulled it on. Ten seconds later, I arrived at Pier 86. I heard the fight before I saw it. I counted five sets of heartbeats. If Goldfinch and what's-his-name were tangling with baddies near the aircraft carrier, they were outnumbered. As I zoomed over Hell's Kitchen, I could make them out visually in the distance. Sure enough, the new guys were faring badly. I don't know what sort of villains they encountered in Peoria, but in New York we grow a special kind of thug.

A huge spool of fiber optic cable provided a great lasso, which I used to wrangle the attackers and secure them. It took a little over a second, and they sat blinking furiously, trying to figure out how the fight they were winning a second earlier had turned so badly against them.

"Far out," the tall guy, Goldfinch, said. Even behind the goggles, I could see a knot on his forehead swelling. A trickle of blood ran down his jaw. The other one—Scarlet Wasp—lay spread-eagled on the ground, snoring softly. "Thanks, Cap! You got here at exactly the right time."

I grabbed him by the front of his costume and lifted him against the wall. His grin contorted into a grimace.

"You told Blade Mistress about Harvey," I said.

"Harvey? Harvey who? Hey, let me down, dude. Chill!"

"Sunburst. You told Blade Mistress that Sunburst was dead."

"Okay."

"So, how did you know? Harvey was an introvert. He didn't like to be around people he'd known for years. There's no way he'd let you get to know him after only a week or so. I figure you know more about how he died than you're letting on, but not because you were friends. How did you know he had died before anyone else?"

"I didn't, man. Let me down. I got no reason to lie to you."

I slid him down the wall. He dusted off his costume, and then he turned around. "Did you scuff it? The back of the suit? Huh? You have any idea how hard it is to keep this costume tidy? It has, like, a million little armor plates. If I get mud or dirt up in there, it takes a week with an old toothbrush to clean it out."

"It looks fine. Tell me about Sunburst."

"What makes you think I knew about him first? Hey, I was just making conversation with Blade Mistress. For a guy from the Great Plains, that's like meeting Mickey Mantle. I was in awe, dude. Have you ever noticed how, because she's like seven feet tall, the only place you can look is her chest?"

I had. "Stay on the subject."

"Oh, yeah. Sure. So, I figured she already knew about Sunburst. That's why I said, *'Hey, you hear about Sunburst?'* I was just making conversation. We're new in town. We don't know a lot of people. I was networking, man."

A few feet away, Scarlet Wasp stirred, groaned, and tried to sit up. He immediately grabbed his head.

"Your buddy has a concussion," I told Goldfinch. "You want to get that looked at. A contra-coup injury is nothing to mess with. Why did you think Blade Mistress must have known already that Harv ... er, Sunburst was dead?"

He told me.

And everything fell into place.

Zandy opened the door before I knocked, again. I was back in the Eddie Shane trench coat and fedora. If I was wrong, no harm done. Nobody would be asking why Captain Courage was hanging around outside a rent-controlled apartment in SoHo.

If I was right, it wouldn't matter what I wore.

Zandy was in the Swift costume.

"Planning on going out tonight?" I asked.

"Blade Mistress is gone. There's a void. Word will get around. It will be a field day for criminals. Someone needs to be out on the streets protecting the populace." She said all of it with minimal emotion.

"You're overwrought," I said. "Let's have a seat and talk about this."

"My duty is clear," she said.

"Yeah. About that. You have another duty, you know. When you learn something critical, you're supposed to tell your partner."

"What?"

"Blade Mistress learned that Harvey was dead from a couple of newbies from Peoria. They told me they heard about Harvey from *you*. I just came from Sam's Heroes Bar. Everybody there told me they heard about Harvey from Blade Mistress. You told Goldfinch and his sidekick, they told Blade Mistress, and Blade Mistress told everyone else. I asked you, earlier tonight, whether you'd discussed Harvey's death with your partner. You said you hadn't, but you knew about it almost before anyone.

That leaves me with the question—who told you?"

"I did," said someone behind me. I'd been so focused on Swift, I hadn't noticed a third heartbeat in the room. As soon as she spoke, I knew who she was. I turned slowly toward her.

"Vicki Valiant," I said.

"Eddie. How's it hangin'? You're overdressed."

"How did you learn about Harvey?" I asked.

"I'm a reporter. We hear things."

I shook my head. "You also report things. A superhero goes down, and it isn't front page news?"

"Not anymore! There're so damned *many* of you these days, when one of them drops dead they're lucky to get an unpaid obituary in the *Times!* It's not like he got taken down by The Minotaur, anyway. He just stroked out. I got a call from a contact down at the morgue. The EMTs cut away Harvey's suit. They thought he was some kind of fetishist. They didn't recognize Sunburst. Poor Harvey. He never was what you'd call a high-profile hero. Could have used better PR. Nobody reported it, because—in this city—nobody cared. Sad."

"Why aren't you composting over in Coney Island?" I asked. "Blade Mistress told me you were flying to Cabo with her tonight."

"Did she? How unfortunate. She was always a little indiscreet. I'm not 'out' to everyone, you know."

"You never intended to go to Cabo."

"A reporter's life is unpredictable. Vacation opportunities are few and far between. Plans change at the last minute. I told her to fly ahead, and I'd catch up tomorrow or the next day."

"You're lying," I said. Her heart rate had jumped ten beats per second, and I could smell the chemical composition of her blood turning acid due to hyperventilation. Physiological arousal is one symptom of lying. She looked into my eyes, and I could see the realization behind them. She was lying. I knew it, and she knew I knew it.

"You didn't expect me to be here tonight," I continued. "You thought you had more time. Why *are* you here, anyway? I told Swift you and Blade Mistress were flying to Mexico together. There was no reason for her to call you to console her over her loss. Therefore, you came here on your own accord. Swift doesn't appear to be alarmed over your resurrection from the dead, and therefore she knew you weren't on the plane."

"Eddie," Swift said, placing a hand on my arm. "Let it go."

"Can't. It's my nature, Sugarcheeks. I got this in my teeth now, and I ain't letting go. Blade Mistress introduced you to Vicki when they started dating. Somewhere along the line, Vicki decided she liked you better than your partner. When she was told Harvey had died, Vicki saw an opportunity to get rid of Blade Mistress and keep you for herself. She begged off the trip to Cabo, sabotaged Blade Mistress's jet, and planned to blame it on one of Blade Mistress's enemies. I bet you already have a rough draft of the headline story on your computer, don't you, Vicki?"

"Of course. As soon as I heard about the crash, I started on it."

"Because you arranged for the crash."

"What if I did? Jeez, the woman was seven freakin' feet tall! She weighed damned near three hundred pounds, and let me tell you, Buster, it was all solid muscle. She had a real anger problem too. If she'd found out about Zandy and me, she'd have pounded me into butter. When I heard about Harvey, and the way he was found in the costume, I decided it was time to act. Is that what you wanted to hear? Sure! I killed Blade Mistress. Are you happy?"

"No," I said. "I'm very sad. But I know someone who *will* be happy."

The door opened, and Detective Tom Holden strode in with two uniformed officers.

"Oh, screw this!" Swift yelped. She vanished in an instant, leaving only a faint electric crackle in the air and the reverberations of a sonic boom in her wake.

"Vicki Valiant, Intrepid Girl Reporter," Tom said. "You are under arrest for the murder of Amazonia Aegea, aka Blade Mistress."

"It's Shane's word against mine," Vicki said, as she struggled vainly against the grasp of the officers. "Whatever he tells you, it's a lie."

I opened my trench coat and showed her the wire Tom had secured there before I came up to the apartment. "Your own words will condemn you, Vicki."

"What about Swift?" Tom asked.

"I'll put in a call to Captain Courage," I said. "He'll find her in a day or so. She can't run forever."

I dragged my heels looking for Zandy. She was a sweet kid, and Vicki Valiant was twice her age, gorgeous, and relentless in getting what she wanted.

Vicki was right. Blade Mistress did have a temper. Maybe Vicki never intended to fall for Swift, but once they crossed the boundaries of fidelity, cheating on Blade Mistress was equivalent to taking a half-gainer into a wood chipper.

So, I gave Swift a head start. Things came up. I had other priorities. Bad guys needed to be caught. She's out there, somewhere.

Maybe she *can* run forever, after all.

THE WILL AND WAYNE SHOW

Adam Chase

Dewey's Diner had a small but loyal clientele. Its food wasn't the greatest, but what it lacked in quality, it made up for in quantity. Its claim to fame was "The Dewey Dig," meaning that every customer could count on having to dig through a pile of fries to find his sandwich. As marketing strategies go, it was genius. New customers were often so busy marveling at the amount of fries heaped on their plates that it never occurred to them to think about whether they were very good.

And then there was the fact that Dewey's had a well-deserved reputation as a survivor. The place had been serving up calories and cholesterol to hungry customers for over fifty years. It had weathered wars, storms, floods, recessions, and even a fire in 1998. Dozens of fancier establishments had come and gone while Dewey's, like Ol' Man River, just kept rolling along.

During the typical lunch shift Dewey's was about three-quarters full. Such was the case on a Thursday when Will Pinkney and Wayne Corbin sauntered in and selected a booth in the back. Thinking themselves hilarious, they had started referring to their friendship as The Will and Wayne Show because just about everything they did, they did together. This included being a two-man team of flooring installers for a couple of local carpet and tile outlets. But their real specialties were getting tats, drinking beer, smoking pot, and ogling women. On this particular day, it was the latter that was on their minds.

The current object of their less-than-wholesome desire was Wendy Crosby. An attractive, newly-divorced single mom, Wendy had recently moved from out of town and taken a job at Dewey's to earn a few extra dollars. Will and Wayne, connoisseurs of the female form that they were, practically dropped down on all fours and barked like dogs the first time they saw her. Slender and tanned, Will thought Wendy looked like Jessica Alba. Wayne quipped that she looked like the future Mrs. Wayne Corbin to him, which set them both to snickering, even though they knew (as did anyone with two functioning eyes) that Wendy was a million miles out of their league.

However, this dichotomy did not stop them from making Dewey's their current go-to spot for lunch. The Will and Wayne Show did not excel at math, but they did manage to figure out that since Dewey's had only two waitresses working the lunch shift, they had a fifty-fifty chance of sliding into a booth that would be serviced by the adorable Ms. Crosby. On those days when they guessed right, they could barely control their excitement.

For her part, Wendy had grown weary of the two losers. The first time she served them they acted a little awkward and shy, but in no time they became more aggressive and even openly rude and sexist with their comments. They called her "babe" and "honey." They openly stared at her chest, often placing their entire order without either of them ever raising their eyes to meet hers. They asked personal questions like where did she live, was she lonely, and since she had a tan line where her wedding ring used to be, did she need a new man. They also told her filthy jokes just to see her reaction. And they stared. No matter where she went in the room, she felt their eyes boring into her like lasers. She served them because she understood that rude customers are just part of the serving gig. But she did it with a clenched jaw, avoiding eye contact, and never, ever answering their personal questions or lingering at their table. Often, she walked away while one of them was talking to her. Still, they kept coming in day after day.

On this particular Thursday, Wendy was delighted to see that The Will and Wayne Show was somewhat distracted by a pair of attractive women (one blonde and the other brunette) who walked into Dewey's and took the booth directly across the aisle from them. The women appeared to be about Wendy's age and, if not quite as good looking, certainly good enough to set off a spark or two in the likes of Will Pinkney and Wayne Corbin. The boys, who couldn't spell *subtlety* let alone define it, gaped openly at the two women, who, like all women Will and Wayne encountered, showed not the slightest shred of interest.

Will had just swallowed the last bite of his burger and belched when the two women's conversation took an interesting turn. Will and Wayne, who had been eavesdropping all along, tuned in even more when they heard this exchange about old Doc Hansford, who lived all alone in a big old house about a mile outside the city limits:

The blonde said to the brunette, "Do you believe he just has small checking and savings accounts at the bank? The man was a doctor for decades and you and I both probably have more money in the bank than he does."

"Are you serious?" the brunette asked.

"Yes, and get this: Mr. Wyman thinks he probably has money hidden all over that house and doesn't even have a security system. I mean, it has to be someplace, doesn't it? I've heard about people who do that, people who don't trust the banks because they were raised during the depression so they hide their money in their houses. And now he's had a heart attack?"

The brunette said, "Yeah, I took care of him yesterday in ICU and he's in rough shape. I wonder what will happen if he doesn't make it. Somebody said his wife died years ago and he doesn't have any kids."

"Wow. Imagine going into that old house after he dies to clean out all the years of accumulated junk and finding piles of money everywhere. I wonder what they would do with it?"

Will and Wayne's eyes were as big as the headlights on a Peterbilt, but somehow they managed to contain themselves until they got to the parking lot where they pooled their powers of deduction and put it all together: The blonde obviously worked at one of the banks in town and the brunette was apparently a nurse at the hospital, putting them in unique positions to know critical facts about the old doctor's business. Specifically, that he was in the hospital, maybe about to die, and that his house was sitting out there in the country empty of people but full of money.

Wayne said to Will, "Dude, you thinkin' what I'm thinkin'?"

Will said, "Are you thinkin' we ought pay a visit to that old man's house and see if we can find some of that money?"

"That's exactly what I'm thinkin'."

"Then, yeah, I'm thinkin' what you're thinkin'."

And with that, The Will and Wayne Show bumped fists and set about the business of planning what would be their first official burglary. They'd both stolen many times, having shoplifted everything from candy bars to clothing, but this would be their first B&E. The idea excited them, especially because it promised to be so easy: A big old house with no close neighbors, no fences, no spotlights, probably no alarm system to circumvent (because most people that old geezer's age are totally old school), and best of all, nobody home. Who could ask for a better opportunity? The place was practically calling out to them, begging them to pay it a visit.

That afternoon, The Will and Wayne Show went back to work and finished their carpet job in half the time it normally would have taken them, partly because they were so energized and partly because they couldn't talk about their plans with the homeowner lurking within earshot. When at last they threw their tools in the back of the truck and drove away, they ran their mouths a hundred miles an hour, mostly talking about the money, how much there might be and what they would each do with their share. Yessiree, The Will and Wayne Show was about to hit the big time.

They settled on the following evening. It would have been smarter to wait a few days and surveille the old house just to make sure no one, either friend or relative, was stopping by to check on things or pick up the mail or even serve as a house sitter. But strategizing was not The Will and Wayne Show's strong suit. They were men of action more than thought, men of impulse more than patience. They did, however, drive around the property that morning and conclude that the best way to keep their truck from being seen near the house was to park in a grove of trees just off the highway a quarter of a mile away, and then walk through a wooded area and approach the house from the back. After identifying just the right spot to hide the truck, they bumped fists and congratulated themselves on their brilliance.

Then they went shopping.

They bought latex gloves, flashlights, and duffle bags to carry the money in. The question they struggled with was how many duffle bags to buy. What if there was so much money it wouldn't fit into two bags? They finally decided to buy six bags. If there was more money than would fit into six bags, they would just have to drive home, empty the bags, and head back to get the rest.

Their final purchases came from the local J.C. Penney. Not being men of fashion, their wardrobe consisted almost entirely of blue jeans and white company-logoed T-shirts. Even Will and Wayne understood that such clothing would not be optimal for the task at hand, so they bought a couple of black long-sleeved pullovers. By the time they were out of the store and back in the truck, their confidence was soaring. If it hadn't still been daylight, they would have sped out to the old house right then. As it was, they had time to kill, so they headed to Dewey's instead.

Wendy saw them push through the door and glanced at her watch. It was two-thirty, a good two-and-a-half hours later than they usually arrived. Unfortunately, it was her day to handle things alone during the slow period between two and four, so she would have to deal with them no matter where they chose to sit. And she had a feeling it would be worse than usual today, judging from the smirks they were wearing. And the swagger. How two complete losers on the very bottom rung of the social ladder could carry themselves with so much swagger was beyond her.

As she approached their table, Will looked right at her chest and said, "Hey, howya doin' sweetcakes? Didya miss us at lunchtime?"

Wendy said, "Oh yeah. I wasn't sure how I was going to make my car payment without those fifty-cent tips."

"Aw, baby, you so mean to us. Here we yo' most loyal customers and you talk to us like we nothin'. Why you do that?"

Wendy ignored his question and readied herself to jot down their orders. "Just tell me what you want."

"What would you say if I told you me and Wayne were gonna be comin' up in the world real soon?"

Wendy said, "Up's the only direction you guys could go."

"Aw, there you go again, hurtin' me and Wayne's tender feelin's. Are your tender feelin's hurt, Wayno?"

"Yup. My feelin's are hurt bad."

"Mine too," Wayne continued, "but someday, sweetheart, when we get ours, you gonna be sorry you were so mean to us."

"I am, huh?" Wendy said.

"Oh yeah. You gonna be hot for The Will and Wayne Show then. You gonna be feelin' little tingles all over when we walk in here. Ain't that right, Wayno?"

"Yup."

Wendy looked at the ceiling and shook her head. "Whatever you say. Now what are you going to have? I need to get back to work."

Twenty minutes later, Will and Wayne dropped their pocket change and a few crumpled bills by their empty plates, noisily sucked the last of their soft drinks down the hatch, and blew kisses to Wendy as they strolled out the door. When she cleared their table and collected their money, she saw that they had stiffed her, probably because of the wisecrack she'd made about their fifty-cent tips. The funny thing was, she didn't even care. She'd rather get no tip at all than have to carry money in her purse that their hands had touched. That's how much she despised them.

The Will and Wayne Show hit the road just about dark. Of course, they shouldn't have been attempting the break-in at all. But if they *were* going to try it, they should have waited until midnight or later to cut down on the number of people on the roads and reduce the risk of being seen. But the buzz of excitement they felt, combined with their inability to think critically, meant that, as usual, patience and sound reasoning would not factor into their choices.

As they approached the spot where they had planned to pull the truck into the stand of trees, Will glanced at his rearview mirror. He saw headlights in the distance, but figured they were too far away to tell that he was turning where there was no road, so he goosed the accelerator and drove over the shoulder and back into the grove as far as he could before killing the headlights.

When the lights went out, things got very real for The Will and Wayne Show. Sudden, total darkness has a way of jolting your senses. It's an abnormal condition that can be disorienting and takes time to adapt to. For a moment, neither Will nor Wayne said anything, ostensibly waiting for the car that had been following them to pass. When it zoomed by a few seconds later, they relaxed a bit.

"It's dark," Wayne said.

"Duh," Will countered. "Ain't it usually dark when the sun goes down?"

"Yeah, but I didn't think it was gonna be *this* dark."

"You feelin' spooked, bro?"

"Naw, I'm just saying it's dark is all."

Will held up his flashlight. "That's why we bought these, Einstein. Come on, let's go."

But the moment they turned the flashlights on they felt conspicuous. Would someone driving by on the highway see the bouncing shafts of light through an opening in the trees? To reduce that possibility, they used only one of the flashlights and kept it pointed at the ground. This meant that their faces were susceptible to being raked by low-hanging branches as they trekked through the woods. Will, who was in the lead, took the brunt of them and had scratches on his forehead and cheek by the time they reached Dr. Hansford's back yard. It crossed his mind that he would have to figure out a way to explain those scratches, but he would worry about that later.

They knelt at the edge of the woods with their bags and gathered their thoughts. The red brick two-story house was at least one hundred years old and seemed bigger up-close than it did from the road. There was also an exterior basement entrance on the back of the house, which meant a total of three stories they might have to search. Neither Will nor Wayne said it, but they were both thinking that there could be a million places to hide money in a place that size, including behind loose bricks, removeable floorboards, and perhaps hundreds of ceiling panels that all looked alike. And what if there was a safe? They'd both been too busy picturing an eccentric old man hiding money under his mattress to consider that he might have a thousand-pound safe bolted to the floor. Suddenly, a job that seemed so easy a few hours ago felt hopeless.

Will knew Wayne well enough to know that, in a few seconds, he would suggest they abort the mission and head back to the car. Wayne was cool, but he was a pessimist at his core, which made him a coward and a quitter when things got hard. Will, on the other hand, saw the same problems but was more of an optimist. He felt suddenly uneasy too, but there was no way he was going to get this far and not go through with what they'd planned. He'd live with regret the rest of his life if he didn't find out what was in that house. He would always wonder if his fortune had been just a few feet away and ripe for the picking.

Will put his hand on Wayne's shoulder and said, "You ready to get rich?"

"I don't know, Will. You really think this is a good idea?"

"No, dude, it's a *great* idea. This is our shot. We ain't never gonna get rich crawlin' around on hard floors. All we gonna get is shot knees by the time we fifty."

"But what if it ain't there or we can't find it?"

"Then we ain't no worse off, are we?"

Wayne thought about this and decided it was true. This likely would be the only time in his miserable life that he would have a chance to get his hands on some real money. He looked at Will and said, "You're right, bro. Let's do it."

And with that, they stood and started toward the house.

They'd brought along a screwdriver to try to jimmy the back door open, but the thing was solid and tight with a lock in the doorknob and a deadbolt about six inches above it. Will told Wayne to stand back, then used the butt of his flashlight to break the glass panel closest to the locks. The sound of shattering glass tore through the quiet night like a cymbal crash, but no lights popped on, nor could any voices or footsteps be heard inside the house. They'd expected the place to be empty, but this confirmed it. With growing confidence, Will reached inside, twisted both the door lock and deadbolt, and pushed the door open.

Glass crunched under their feet as they stepped into the house and closed the door behind them. Their twin flashlight beams, dancing and criss-crossing in the darkness, told them they were in the kitchen, and a large, fancy one at that. But they had already decided that the money probably wouldn't be in the kitchen. Too much danger of some unsuspecting person rooting through drawers and cabinets in search of just the right spoon or skillet or exotic spice and finding it by accident. No, it would be hidden better than that, perhaps stashed in an attic crawlspace or stuffed into a mattress. The Will and Wayne Show had seen lots of movies and knew that kitchens were never where people hid their money.

To their right was an arched doorway gaping at them like the entrance to a cave. Huddled close together, they stepped through it onto some luxuriously soft carpet. Before them sat a huge mahogany table directly underneath what looked in their flashlight beams to be a crystal chandelier. It was surrounded by six high-back chairs with ivory-colored satiny padded seats that perfectly matched an elaborate floral centerpiece. Will and Wayne, accustomed as they were to eating fast food straight out of the sack or frozen dinners off of their laps on the couch, could only whistle and mutter expletives as they took in a level of elegance that seemed to them to be other worldly.

From there, they moved through another doorway into a large living room. Wayne's flashlight beam landed on a large red-brick fireplace with a gigantic television hung over the mantel, while Will's explored the angles of the plush pillow-laden sectional sofa that was positioned in front of it.

"Ain't no doubt about it," Wayne said. "This cat is loaded."

That's when they heard the unmistakable sound of a racking shotgun.

And then another.

One behind them and one in front.

Will said, "What the ..." just as the lights came on and revealed the extent of the predicament in which they found themselves. In front of them stood the blonde that had sat across from them at the diner, and behind them stood her brunette companion. The bank employee and the nurse, the ones who'd been so full of speculation about the money hidden in this house, had them covered with shotguns that had muzzles the size of railroad tunnels.

"If you move, you're dead," the blonde said.

"Drop the bags and take a seat," the brunette said.

The boys didn't have to be told twice.

And then a third voice from their left: "I see you've met my sisters."

It was Wendy Crosby, who only seven hours ago had served them a meal at Dewey's. Wendy Crosby, whom they'd been intentionally annoying and disrespecting and harassing for weeks. Wendy Crosby, who'd been the object of their fantasies and was now the orchestrator of their worst nightmare. Having her hair pulled back and wearing jeans and a sweatshirt made her look completely different. That and the fact that she was holding a pistol instead of a plate of food.

"We wondered if you morons would try to break into Grandpa's house if you knew he was in the hospital and thought he had a pile of cash hidden here. Marie and

Jenny didn't think you'd be that stupid, but I see you just about every day and I said, 'Oh, trust me ... they're that stupid.' So they came in and sat in the booth across from you and played their little part and you fell for it. I could tell from watching your eyes as you eavesdropped on their conversation that you were swallowing it hook, line, and sinker."

Will and Wayne, who had lived their lives without a speck of self-awareness, suddenly and for the first time felt like the idiots they were. Sitting there in their new pullovers and latex gloves with empty duffle bags at their feet, they could only stare at the floor like chastened ten-year-olds being lectured by their parents.

"But don't worry, guys," Wendy continued. "When you get to jail I'm sure you can find someone to bully. May I suggest the three-hundred pounder with prison tats and the ring in his nose? I'd love to see how your schtick works on him."

Just then, the sound of sirens began to swell in the distance.

Wendy said, "In case you're wondering, that's your escort service coming to pick you up and take you to your new digs. I called them from an upstairs bedroom as soon as you broke the glass in the back door."

Will leaned forward and put his face in his hands.

Wayne stared at the floor and looked like he was about to cry.

Wendy grinned at her sisters and said, "Nice work, girls. The Will and Wayne Show has officially been canceled."

MURDERER'S PARADISE

Michael Mallory

"Tony Farland!" a voice cried behind him. "I was hoping you'd be here!"

"In the bathroom?" Tony replied, standing at a urinal in the palatial men's room of the historic Egyptian Theatre in Hollywood.

Phil Brodie laughed. "At the show, I mean," he said. "I figured a retro double-feature of *Return of the Zombie* and *The Ape Man's Revenge* would be enough to draw you away from your computer."

Brodie and Farland were both in the same racket—film history—though Tony had the higher profile, being the author of a handful of books on Hollywood's golden age and a frequent talking head for DVD extras. It was, however, not lucrative enough to quit the day job, which was as a researcher for the Motion Picture Academy. Brodie was more of an academic, teaching film at UCLA in between writing articles for fan magazines.

After Tony washed and dried his hands, Brodie said, "Let's go somewhere we can talk in private." They found a corner of the courtyard that was empty.

"If you want me to speak to your class again, you could just email me," Tony said.

"No, it's not that. This is big, real big."

"Okay, Phil, what is it?"

"They found *Murderer's Paradise*."

Now Tony was interested. "A print of it?"

"No, not a print ... they found the *internegative*."

"Good God!"

The 1955 crime drama *Murderer's Paradise* was one of the most notable of all lost films ... at least for movie buffs. Produced independently by Leonard Loesch, the eccentric heir to an oil fortune who decided he wanted to be in the picture business, it was never actually released to theatres. The erratic producer held the film back, keeping it under wraps because, it was claimed, he was unhappy with the ending but could not figure out a better one. Hollywood legend had it that the producer, who was then coming to the end of his moviemaking career, destroyed every print and all the materials from the picture.

"I'm not telling everybody about the interneg yet," Brodie went on. "I first want to drum up interest in the print."

"Where was all this found?" Tony said.

"You know Loesch's old headquarters building in Hollywood? Some repair work was being done there, and the workmen discovered a room nobody knew existed. It was filled with film reel cans, and included the negative for *Murderer's Paradise*. I got a call by the owner of the building last month and went to check it out. It's there, Tony. It really exists."

The expression on Brodie's face—that of a kid who just opened up a birthday present expecting underwear, and getting a PS5 instead—caused Farland to grin.

"Phil, you know what often happens when a legendary lost film is finally found. Once the excitement over the discovery dies down, the thing is screened and people realize that maybe it should have stayed lost."

"We can both be the judge of that. A print is being struck even as we speak and I'm going to set up a private screening and I want you to come."

"When?"

"Next Thursday night at the Westwood Preview House. It will be only for film historians and critics."

"Count me in," Tony said.

Further elaboration about the discovery of the film appeared in an above-the-fold article in the *Daily Variety* two days later, in which Phil Brodie was extensively quoted. But there was no mention of the screening.

In the days prior to the event, Farland found himself getting more and more excited about it, so much so that when the day came, he cursed the abominable L.A. traffic that threatened to make him late. When he approached the screening theatre, though, his heart sank.

An armada of police and emergency vehicles were parked in front of Westwood Preview House, lights flashing.

Finding a place to park (which wasn't easy), Farland ran to the building, just in time to see a body being wheeled out on a gurney. The first person he recognized was Bernard Melton, who was the best-known film historian in the country. Like most others, Tony had grown up reading Melton's books, which he started writing barely out of high school.

"Bernard, what the hell's going on?" he asked.

"The screening's been cancelled, Tony, and so has Phil," Melton deadpanned.

"What?"

"That's him on the gurney. They say he was murdered."

"Good God. Who did it?"

"Obviously, they don't know yet. But whoever it was should be easy to catch since they'll be lugging around projection reels of film."

Farland looked at him with an uncomprehending expression.

"The print of *Murderer's Paradise* was stolen as well," Melton said. "I always hate trying to predict what's going to happen in a story, Tony, but I don't think this was a spur-of-the-moment crime."

The police did not think so either. All of the invitees to the screening, as well as the screening room staff, were gathered in the auditorium for general questioning, which was done by an LAPD detective named Charleston. African American, short, stocky, and balding, he looked more like Tony's middle school science teacher than a policeman.

"I assume all of you knew the deceased," the detective began, standing in front of the stage.

Heads bobbed, though only Bernard Melton spoke. "I can't say I knew him well, Detective. He was more of an acquaintance, someone I saw at functions and events."

"How about the rest of you?"

Tony spoke up. "I think Bernard summed it up perfectly. Phil had a wide range of acquaintances, but I've never met anyone who claimed to have known him intimately."

That prompted another round of nodding and muttered agreement.

"Can you tell us how Phil was killed, Detective?" asked Melton.

"Obviously, we won't know conclusively until after the autopsy," Charleston replied, "though I don't think the bullet hole in his chest helped his condition. Anyone here carry a gun?"

"Only in our dreams," said Tessa Pérez, an L.A. film critic, which provoked a low rumble of chuckles.

"Mind if I ask when Phil was killed?" Tony inquired.

"The projectionist came in about 6:30," Charleston replied. "He's the one who found the body."

"Thank heavens for that."

"I'm sorry?"

"What I mean is, the rest of us here didn't arrive until seven or after, for a 7:30 screening. We all signed in out front. You can check the times on the sheet. That should tell you that none of us could have done this."

Charleston smiled, looking a bit like a snake eyeing a gathering of hamsters. "Unless one or more of you arrived earlier, found the front door unlocked, came in, killed him, took the film, and then came back officially," he said. "But look, for the time being, let's say you're right. All of you can go, though only after you leave your contact information on the way out."

As he made his way out of the theatre, Farland noticed that a group of people remained, which he assumed were the staff of the theater, except for a tanned, professionally-dressed woman who approached Detective Charleston and began to grill him on police efforts to find the missing film print.

The murder made the next day's news, which downplayed the missing film print, or at least its importance. Tony had a hard time keeping his mind on his work throughout the day, so when the call came in on his cell, he did not have to drop anything to take it.

"Mr. Farland," said a woman's voice, "my name is Daria Street. I work for a law firm that represents the Leonard Loesch Corporation."

"Were you by any chance at the screening last night?" Tony asked, remembering a striking woman talking to the police.

"The non-screening, you mean? Yes, I was there. When I heard about the film's discovery, I insisted on being present."

"What can I do for you, Ms. Street?"

"I've been told you can give me a lot of information about the film."

"What sort of questions do you have?"

"Quite a few, actually. Unfortunately, what I don't have right now is time, so I was hoping we could schedule a meeting."

"When?"

"Well, would it be possible to meet for dinner tonight?" she asked. "Do you know Luigi's in Hollywood?"

"On Las Palmas? Sure." Luigi's was an old-style Italian restaurant that had been in Hollywood since the forties. It had even been used in a few movies.

"I'll see you there at 7:30."

Tony Farland set aside what he was supposed to be working on and went down to the library vaults to do a little private research before his dinner date.

Getting his first good look at Daria Street, Farland thought she appeared much less formidable than when she was confronting a police detective. She was tall, slender woman with short chestnut hair, who might have been anywhere from thirty to fifty. He suspected the first, though she projected the natural authority of someone closer to the latter. She smiled upon seeing him and headed for his booth.

"Thank you for agreeing," she said, shaking his hand and sliding across from him. "My firm will pay."

"Oh, you don't ..."

"Yes, I do. Order anything you like."

As she perused the menu, Daria Street said, "I imagine you're wondering why I contacted you instead of someone like Bernard Melton."

"It had crossed my mind," Tony said. "Then after we spoke, it hit me." He reached beside him and picked up a manila envelope, which he plopped on the table. "Everything I could find in the Academy files on *Murderer's Paradise*. My access to these files was why, I presume, you called me instead of Bernard."

"Very perceptive," she said, smiling and picking up the envelope. "May I keep this?"

"Yes. They're copies, and I won't even charge you a quarter a page."

"You can if you like. I have an expense account. In the meantime, could you give me coverage on the material in here?"

"Well, Elliot Brent and Martha Quinlan were the film's stars, second raters both, which probably meant *Murderer's Paradise* was destined to flop from the onset. But in typical Loesch fashion, he kept ordering retakes and rewrites, which ballooned the budget and greatly lengthened the schedule. Finally the original director, Joseph McCully, quit and Loesch took over himself, like he'd done in the past. But in the past he'd not been quite so crazy. Oh, sorry."

Daria Street smiled wanly. "I represent the company, not Loesch's estate. Go on."

"There's not much else to say. The majority of the press coverage at the time was about cost overruns and scheduling problems, supporting roles being recast, and the like. Then the film was destroyed, and it didn't seem like anyone missed it. If not for film buffs like us who conduct interviews with old timers who have occasionally mentioned it, people wouldn't even know the thing ever existed."

"Is the print of the film worth a lot of money?" she asked.

"To a collector it might be," he replied. "Then again, since the interneg was found, any number of new prints could be struck."

"The what?"

"The internegative, the dupe negative from which all prints are made. Phil told me that's what had been found, not simply a print."

Daria Street pulled out a pad and pen, and jotted the word down. "Where is it?" she asked.

"Whatever lab was used to strike the positive, I would imagine."

At that moment the waiter came to their table, but instead of ordering, Daria Street pulled out a fifty-dollar bill, placed it on the table, and slid out of the bench.

"Was it something I said?" Farland asked.

"No, I just remembered something I need to do," she replied. "Thanks for this material. We'll be in touch."

After watching her leave the restaurant, Tony turned to the waiter and said, "I'll have the lasagna and a glass of red ... Sangiovese if you have it."

"Of course," the waiter said, leaving Tony Farland alone and puzzled.

Two days later Tony received a call in his office telling him that a policeman was waiting to see him in the lobby. Both eager and anxious, he went down and spotted Detective Charleston standing by the bust of Douglas Fairbanks. "Thanks for seeing me, Mr. Farland," Charleston said. "Are you familiar with a company called Format Labs?"

"Sure," Tony said. "It's one of the bigger film processing labs in town. Why?"

"Someone broke in there last night and stole something."

"Let me guess ... the negative of *Murderer's Paradise*."

There was a long pause before the detective said, "Funny how you should know that."

"I didn't know, I'm simply speculating. Phil Brodie told me the negative existed, and he had a print struck from it for the screening that didn't happen, so if there was a robbery at a processing lab, it stands to reason it would be the one holding the interneg."

"How many people knew the negative was there?"

"That I don't know. Phil said he was keeping the existence of the negative secret, but if he told me about it. ... I in turn told the lawyer from the Loesch Company. Beyond that, who knows?"

"Do you know someone named Rick McCully?"

"McCully? Well, the director of *Murderer's Paradise* was Joseph McCully, so I'm assuming it's a relative," Tony said. "Have you spoken with him?"

"No, we found his name on a piece of scratch paper in the victim's workplace. Do you know how to get in touch with him?"

"Until now I didn't know he existed. Don't you have databases and things like that?"

"Of course," Charleston replied, "but nothing shows up under either Rick or Richard."

"I'll tell you what ... I'll pull all of the files on Joseph McCully and see if the name Rick turns up anywhere."

"I'd appreciate it."

As soon as the detective left, Tony went into the records room and pulled the bio and clippings files on Joseph McCully, whom he discovered had died in 1992 at 73. If Rick McCully was his son, he'd have to be getting up there. In the bio file he found a studio fact sheet written sometime in the 1950s that gave the name Lucinda as his daughter, but did not mention a son.

He then worked his way through the clippings file and was about to acknowledge defeat when he came to a tiny snip that had been taped to an index card, detailing that a defamation lawsuit had been filed against the author of a book about Hollywood rumors and secrets that mentioned an unsavory scandal connected to director Joseph McCully. The plaintiff, according to the account, was the late director's grandson, Derrick McCully.

Derrick ... *Rick*.

Tony knew immediately getting back to Charleston with this information was the right thing to do, but it was unlikely the detective would be back at his desk yet. So he Googled Derrick McCully and found a site listing him as a teacher at something called the Hollywood Motion Picture Academy.

Cute, Tony thought.

Dialing the number offered on the site, Tony was automatically connected to a machine. He left his number, but no specific message. By end of day, though, no one had called him back. Tony packed up his briefcase and left to go home. Halfway there his iPhone rang. He slid it out of his pocket, holding it under the dash, so a passing police car couldn't see it and ticket him, and hit the *speaker* function. "Hi, this is Tony, and you're making me break the law," he said.

"Tony, it's Daria."

"I already know about the interneg being stolen," he said. "Detective Charleston came by my workplace."

"What are you doing this evening?"

"Well, TCM is showing *All Through the Night*. That's all I had planned. Why?"

"Before the negative was taken, I asked the lab to make a new print and then transfer everything to a DVD. I have it, and I want you to see it. Where can we meet?"

"If you want you can come to my place. I have a player."

"That will work," she replied.

After giving her his address and setting the time, Tony cut off the line.

Daria Street arrived at his small house in the south residential area of Hollywood a little after seven. She looked nervous. "I don't know what's going on," she said, "but I feel like I'm carrying a live grenade in my pocket."

After ushering her in, Tony said, "Have you had dinner? If not, I can call for take-out."

"Chinese sounds good. I'll pay."

When the food situation was arranged, Tony Farland took the disc from her and slipped it into to his DVD player. "Have you watched this yet?" he asked.

"No. But I know it's not only the movie. A separate film can was found containing outtakes and background footage."

"Okay, let's see what we've got," Tony said, taking the disc and slipping it into his player.

Murderer's Paradise was by no means the worst noir crime drama Tony had seen, but was not particularly good, either. Stars Elliot Brent and Martha Quinlan were woodenly adequate, the photography was appropriately shadowy, and the action well handled. It was also short: seventy-two minutes from title to closing credit. But there was nothing Farland could see in the film that was worth murdering anyone over. Their dinner arrived about thirty minutes into it, and they ate while continuing to watch.

When it was over, Daria asked, "Do we need to see it again?"

"I doubt it would make any difference," Tony replied. "What else did you say was on this disc?"

"Outtakes. They should be coming up next."

Farland pressed *Play* again and a series of scenes, completely with clapper boards and crew sounds, appeared. Some were failed takes of shots in the movie, while others were scenes that had been cut out. In the middle of one, Leonard Loesch himself loped on camera to adjust the way his female star Martha Quinlan was standing.

When those ended, what appeared to be a silent travelogue of the city of Los Angeles began to run. It showed traffic on city streets, from behind a moving car, and then cut to side views of the same streets. "Is this location scouting?" Daria asked.

"These must be process plates," Tony said. "It's the footage that's rear-projected on a screen behind the actors sitting in a car, so it looks like they're actually doing the driving. If you're lucky and the lighting's right, it looks convincing. I actually love watching these things. It shows the city the way it was decades ago before it got over crowded and over built. Notice how short the trees are? Most weren't even planted until the nineteen-twen ... hey, what was that?"

"What was what?" Daria asked.

"I just saw something." Tony backed up the start of the sequence and watched again, more intently. When the footage got to the place that had attracted Tony's attention, he froze the picture. "There," he said, pointing to a corner of the screen.

"What are we looking for?" Daria asked.

Progressing frame at a time, a dark, moving shape came into view. It was something falling. While blurred in some frames, in others it was clearly revealed to be a human figure, one that was plummeting down in front of an office building. After advancing a couple dozen more frames, it hit the sidewalk.

"My God!" Daria Street cried.

"Whoever it was must have fallen from the top of that building," Tony said, resuming play. Suddenly the camera car was stopped and a man appeared on camera running toward the figure on the sidewalk. Before he got to it, though, another man appeared, one in a dark suit and hat who emerged from the front door of the building. Seeing him, the presumed cameraman turned and headed back toward the car, while the other man chased him. The cameraman disappeared from view, but the other man reached inside his coat and pulled out a gun.

The picture jostled, indicating that the cameraman had jumped back into the vehicle, but the film still rolled. The second man came close enough to the lens for his lean, hard face to be recognized. He was waving the gun and shouting something, but no sound was being recorded. Finally the camera car took off and sped around a corner. Then the film ended.

"That had to be part of the movie," Daria said. "It must have been cut out."

"I don't think so," Tony replied. "I recognize the man with the gun. It's Charlie Simoneli, a well-connected mobster of the time who was the boyfriend of a blonde bombshell named Abby Parton."

"You're a gangster buff too?"

"Well, back in the forties there wasn't much of a line between the mob and Hollywood. I guess now we know what was in *Murderer's Paradise* that's so dangerous it can't be released, even today. The special effects cameraman caught an actual murder on screen."

"What do we do with this?" Daria asked.

"More research," Tony said.

A stalled car on the 101 meant it took longer than normal for Tony Farland to get to Woodland Hills, where the Motion Picture Country Home was located. The home and attached hospital had been around for eighty years or more, and was open to anyone who had worked within the film industry. Some of Hollywood's best and brightest had spent their final days at the home, and among the current residents was 93-year-old Abby Parton. After parking at the facility, Tony went into the office and asked for directions to Abby Parton's apartment.

"Is she expecting you?" the woman at the desk asked.

"Oh, yes," he fibbed.

Picking up the phone, the woman pressed in a number and said, "Ms. Parton? Someone is here to see you. All right." After clicking off the call, the woman pulled a line-drawn map of the facility, circled a wing, and then drew a line from the office to it before handing it to Farland. Following the map through what looked like a small, landscaped town, he came upon the correct building and went to the suite number he'd been given, then knocked on the door. "Come in," a woman's voice said.

Abby Parton still had the striking facial bone structure she'd been known for during her career. Her formerly red hair was now white gossamer, but her eyes were as clear and blue in person as they appeared in Technicolor. Using a cane to approach Farland, she suddenly stopped, an expression of confusion on her face. "I thought you were going to be my grandson," she said. "Who are you?"

"Ma'am, my name is Tony Farland and I'm from the Academy."

"Have I been expelled?"

"No, nothing like that. I'm just working on a project and I was hoping I might be able to talk to you about it."

"I am retired, you know."

"Yes, I know. This isn't a film project, it's a ... well, it's for a thing I'm writing."

Her eyes narrowed as she said, "I see. Well, come on in then. I have to sit down. My hip, you know." She directed him to sit on a small sofa while she took an old-fashioned winged chair set prominently in the center of the living room. "What is it you're writing about?" she asked.

"It's about the film *Murderer's Paradise*."

She glared at him, and then in a voice twenty degrees colder, said, "I was not in that one."

"I know. But we have evidence that someone you knew was on the set. Charlie Simoneli."

"He was never on the set."

"But he is in the film. At least he showed up in one of the outtakes."

"That was so long ago," Abby Parton sighed.

"I know. But someone was recently killed because they attempted to show a print of that film."

The gaze she leveled at Tony froze him even further. "There are no prints of that film."

"There was one, but it was stolen during the murder," Tony informed her. "I've seen both the film and the outtake ... a process plate, actually. A murder was caught on camera very clearly in the process footage, though it's a lot harder to see in the finished film. Charlie Simoneli, however, also shows up clearly in the background footage."

"What is it you want from me?"

"Any information you have about the murder. You were, after all, Charlie Simoneli's girl at the time."

Abby Parton put one bony hand over the emergency alert button she wore on a chain around her neck. "Young man, whoever you are, if I press this it will take exactly five seconds for a nurse to come in and see what is wrong. When I tell her you are threatening me, it will take another ten seconds for a very large, very strong guard to remove you."

"Ma'am, I'm not—"

"I suggest you leave under your own power while you have the chance."

"I'm sorry to have bothered you, Ms. Parton," Tony said, heading for the door. Before he let himself out, he turned back and added, "But a man I knew was murdered because of this."

Getting back to the lobby of the facility, he saw a thirty-something man standing at the reception desk and gesturing wildly. "You just let some stranger go back there, and you don't know who he was?" the man was shouting.

"Please, sir," the receptionist said, trying to deflect the attack, "I called your grandmother first, and she said it was all right."

"Next time call *me*!" he snarled, storming toward the door to the facility grounds.

Farland turned his face away quickly and tried to make himself small as the man strode past. Tony knew it had to be Abby Parton's grandson, whom she was expecting when he arrived at her door.

What both startled and surprised him—what he couldn't explain—was the fact that, except for longer, lighter hair, the agitated man could have been a photo double for Charlie Simoneli.

"You think our killer is related to the murderer shown in the film?" Daria Street was asking over lunch at Greenblatt's Deli the next day.

"The man certainly looked like him, particularly around the eyes," Tony said. "He's either related or I've got Simoneli on the brain and it's causing me to see things. The problem is I can't find any record that Abby Parton ever had a child, which would be something of a requirement to have a grandson."

"If she and Simoneli were an item, maybe they had an illegitimate child and put it up for adoption."

"That's possible, especially since she was still a star at the time, and in the age of studio morals clauses, starts didn't admit to having children out of wedlock."

"Do you know if Simoneli is still alive?"

"He died in 1974. There's no record of his having a family either."

"So where do we go from here?"

"I'd say going to the police with that disc of outtakes is a good place to start."

"I don't think I made a very good impression on that policeman the other day," Daria admitted. "Maybe you should take it to him." She opened her purse and pulled out the DVD.

"You trust me with this?" he asked.

"Looks like I have to," she said, handing over the disc.

Later, back at work, Tony Farland placed a call to Detective Charleston, but got no further than his answering machine. Speaking quietly so as not to have to explain what he was doing to anyone who might be listening, he gave a brief overview of what he and Daria had discovered, and asked to set up a time when he could pass along the disc. So when the phone rang, he assumed it was Charleston calling him back. He was wrong.

"Mr. Farland," a voice said at the other end of the line, "my name's Rick McCully, and—"

"Mr. McCully! I'm so glad you called back."

"Sorry it took so long, but what's going on? I just got through talking to the police, and telling them I didn't know anything about a screening of my grandfather's old film."

As concisely as he could, Tony Farland brought him up to speed on the case so far, pausing only to answer Rick McCully's requests for reiteration. When he was finished, McCully said, "So you're saying an actual murder was captured on film and nobody realized it at the time?"

"Someone must have, because the film was destroyed ... or so it was believed. Is it possible your grandfather had any indication of the crime?"

"You have to understand that I was only four when he died, so it's not like we had many conversations about his career. I only became interested in his work later."

"Did he leave any papers?"

"Most of those have been donated to libraries."

"Would it be possible to speak to your mother?"

"My mother?"

"I found a document listing a woman named Lucinda as his daughter."

"My mother died of cancer three years ago."

"Oh ... I'm sorry."

"Look, Mr. Farland, I don't really understand much about this, but I have some letters and things of grandfather's, so if I come across anything pertinent, I'll contact you."

After hanging up, Tony tried to go back to work, but it was hard to concentrate. By the end of the day Detective Charleston had not called him back. Tony thought about swinging by the police station and dropping the disc off for him, but he was afraid it would get lost or misplaced. Besides, he wanted to be there when the policeman screened it, so he could point out the pertinent shots.

Just as Tony was about to leave, his phone rang and it was *d*éjà vu all over again: expecting Charleston, he got Rick McCully.

"After we spoke, I went through some of those letters I was telling you about," McCully said, "and I found something I think you should see. Can you come to the Hollywood Motion Picture Academy tonight? It's where I work. They have all sorts of equipment, so bring your disc."

"All right," Tony said. "By the way, you do know that 'Hollywood Motion Picture Academy' is perilously close to the name of my establishment, the real Academy, don't you?"

"I didn't name the place, I just teach here."

McCully gave him directions and Tony promised to be there by 7:30.

After stopping off at a 1950s retro burger joint in Hollywood for dinner, Tony drove to the squat, black, commercial building on Sunset Boulevard whose banner proudly boasted it to be "L.A.'s Finest Film School." He just bet. "Film schools" popped up in Hollywood with the frequency of weeds on a lawn, and rarely lasted long enough to turn out graduates. After parking in the small, mostly empty lot, he made his way through the unlocked door into the lobby, which was empty. A hand-lettered sign on the receptionist desk read, *Tony Farland, please go to Studio C*, and then an arrow pointed the way.

Studio C was an ordinary room with the walls and floor painted green and some lights hung from a metal pipe grid on the ceiling. A video camera sat on a tripod in the middle of the room. This space could have been in somebody's garage, but filmmaking was changing at such warp speed that it hardly mattered. Entire features were being made on smartphones, and given the three-wall green-screen, he imagined that a few pushes of a button were all that stood between him standing in a small room in an office building and a digital Monument Valley.

Tony patted his blazer pocket to make certain the disc was still there, but then he was struck by a thought—*had he ever mentioned to Rick McCully that he had the footage on a DVD*? Thinking back, he thought not.

So how did McCully know?

"Mr. Farland," a voice called, but Tony didn't see anyone.

"Yes, it's me."

"Good."

Now Tony realized there was a small, glassed-in control booth in the back of the room, and he could see a shadow moving inside it. When the figure came out through a door and stepped into the light, he could not suppress a gasp.

It was Abby Parton's grandson.

How had he not recognized the voice when he spoke with the man over the phone?

Because he wasn't screaming over the phone, he thought. People's voices always sounded different when they screamed.

Since Tony had hidden himself from the man at the Country Home, McCully did not show signs of recognizing him as he walked up and shook his hand. "Thanks for coming," McCully said. "You have the disc?"

"I do," Tony replied. "But first, let me ask how your grandmother is doing."

"My grandmother?"

"Abby Parton."

McCully smiled, a reptilian expression that Tony found more discomfiting than his angry face at the facility. "She's fine, though your appearance there did upset her."

"How is it possible that you're the grandson of both Abby and Joseph McCully, and also related to Charlie Simoneli?"

"Why do you say I'm related to Charlie Simoneli?"

"Because I have eyes. You look like him."

McCully's smile broadened. "I actually played him in one of those dopey non-union crime recreation shows a few years ago," he said. "The first time Grandmother saw me, she thought I was Charlie's ghost. But to answer your question, my mother was Abby and Charlie's daughter, born out of wedlock. From what I understand, Abby didn't want the scandal and Charlie didn't want a child. So she was put up for adoption. The people I consider my real grandparents, Joseph and Margie McCully, took her in, under the table, you understand. Leonard Loesch pulled whatever strings it took to facilitate the arrangement with minimal paperwork."

"Why was Loesch involved?" Tony asked, now more fascinated than frightened.

"Well, all concerned parties were dealing with a problem at that time. Loesch and my adoptive grandfather were sitting on a film that incriminated my real grandfather for murder, which Loesch wanted to release, using the on-camera murder angle for publicity. That's the kind of lunatic he was, but when you're that rich, nobody's going to lock you up. It was actually Loesch himself who found a solution to all the problems. He'd heard my grandfather complain that they couldn't have kids, so he proposed Abby give them hers. He facilitated the swap, so to speak, with no one else looking, then destroyed the film, and everybody was happy."

"Wait," Tony said. "I get that Charlie and Abby were happy to be rid of a baby, and Joseph and his wife were happy to get it, and Charlie was happy in the thought that *Murderer's Paradise* was no more, but what did Loesch get out of the deal? He didn't want to destroy the film, after all."

"No, he didn't want to, but Charlie's threat to send certain photos of Loesch and a fifteen-year-old girl that were in his possession to *Confidential* Magazine, if the film was not destroyed, was a strong negotiating ploy. The price for everyone's happiness was that they never say a word about what was captured on film. By the way, the actual cameraman and driver of the camera car each got a chunk of money and the hell scared out of them if they ever talked."

"But you found out somehow. Did your mother tell you this?"

"No. My mom never said a word, and my dad never knew. He died in Afghanistan when I was a kid. But right before she died, Mom revealed that she'd been adopted. I started searching for my mother's birth family and found Abby."

"Sorry, but how? You said there was minimal paperwork regarding the adoption."

"I had help from a private source with private records," McCully said. "You can come out now, Dar."

From somewhere in the back of the room, Daria Street sashayed into the light.

Tony Farland's stomach sank. "I'm really screwed, aren't I?" he uttered.

"You've no idea," she said, pointing a handgun at him.

"Was that club on the head really necessary?" Tony asked upon coming to on the floor.

"It's much easier to tie up an unconscious man," Daria Street said. "Besides, I had the kind of day at work that made me want to pistol-whip my supervisor, but I can't. You were handy, so ..."

"Great," Tony muttered. "I'm glad I could help." Now he realized his wrists had been bound together behind him. His ankles were similarly bound. "What are you planning to do with me?"

"Probably the same thing we did to your friend, Brodie," Rick McCully said.

"I get your involvement, Rick. I don't like it, but I get it. But how are you involved in all this, Daria?"

She pulled a plastic chair over to where he was lying and sat down. "Do you know what the Bar-S Club is?"

"A Western ranch?" Tony guessed.

"It's short for Hollywood Bar-Sinister Club," Daria said. "The members are the descendants of bastard children of celebrities. Some of our membership would astonish you. Big names. Oscar winners."

"No doubt. So who's your daddy, sugar?"

Daria sneered at him, and then said, "My grandpa was Leonard Loesch. My grandma was his nurse."

"And you two are working together to protect the reputations of your forebears, even if it means killing people?"

"We work together in a lot of different ways," McCully said, stepping to Daria and caressing her face.

"We met at a Bar-S meeting," she said, "and one thing led to another."

"Daria, look at me," Tony said, struggling to a seated position. "Why did you pretend to help with the investigation if you were in on the murder?"

"I needed to know what could be discovered about the film, and you seemed like the best one to do it. The business about that negative, for instance. I didn't know anything about that until you told me. I thought they'd only found an old print of the movie. I think that bastard Brodie didn't want me to know so he could control how many prints were made and where they went."

"But it was you who showed me the process footage of the murder and even gave me the disc to pass on to the police," Tony said. "It doesn't make sense."

She smiled. "That DVD I gave you? It has nothing on it but some old newsreels. The police would have written you off as a nutcase, which would have made them more apt to believe *you* were the murderer and thief."

"Yet here I am bound up and held at gunpoint instead of being grilled by a police detective. What made you change your plan?"

"You went to see Abby," McCully answered. "She was upset enough when I told her the film had been found, and then on top of that, you went to see her and questioned her about it. That was a clear indication you weren't going to stop investigating on your own, and you might just figure things out before we could put the frame around you. We had to stop you."

Farland lay back down on the floor. "Since you two are so chatty, mind telling me who it was that was murdered on camera?"

"A business rival of my grandfather's," McCully said. "Abby knows his name."

"Which makes her an accessory after the fact," Daria added. "There's no statute of limitations on murder."

"And I'm not about to let her go to trial at her age," McCully added. "I love her."

"I don't think I've ever been loved by someone so much they'd commit murder on my behalf," Tony said.

"There's a business aspect to this too," Daria said. "Do you have any idea what the future of the Loesch Organization would look like if it was revealed that Leonard not only knew about the murder, but he shelved the film and remained quiet about it solely to avoid his statutory rape from being made public? Stock-wise, we'd be as viable as Enron, and every woman who ever met Leonard Loesch would come forward with a similar accusation, real or imagined."

"So you're just going to shoot me here?" Tony said, hoping to play for more time. "Won't that look a little suspicious when they find my body, all trussed up and executed?"

"Will you really care after your dead?" Daria said.

"What about my car then?"

"What about it?" McCully asked.

"Are you just going to leave it in the parking lot for the police to find? There were a lot of suspects for Brodie's death. I was one initially, and so were you, Daria. But if you kill me here, it won't take the cops long to learn that Rick works here, and probably less time to turn up your involvement with him."

"He has a point," McCully said. "Maybe we haven't thought this through well enough."

"Don't go limp on me now!" she barked. "I need to think." After a half-minute of agonizing silence, she finally said, "He's right. It's too dangerous to do it here. We have to go somewhere else."

"The photo lab?" McCully asked.

"I have a connection there too," she said. "How about that screening room where you offed Brodie? Maybe the cops will think it was someone connected to the place itself."

"That works," McCully said.

"Okay, sit him up and cut the ties. I'll keep the gun on him."

Pulling out a small knife, Rick McCully cut the nylon zip ties that he'd used to bind Farland's hands and feet. Immediately Tony felt the rush of blood flowing warmly back into them.

"Now, get up, slowly," Daria said, pointing the gun at his throbbing head.

"Give me a moment, okay?" Tony begged. "Being clubbed and hogtied takes a little out of one."

Then he looked over at the video camera, which sat placidly on the tripod. "Huh," he uttered.

"Huh what?" Daria said.

"A red light on a camera means it's on, right? I mean, it's a sign that it's recording?"

"Yeah," McCully replied. "Why?"

"Because history's repeating itself. You're filming my attempted murder, just like the process plate photographer filmed your grandfather's crime sixty years ago. That camera's red light is on."

"*What*?" McCully screamed, now sounding like he did at the Country Home. He ran to the camera, as did Daria Street ... which is what Tony was hoping for.

Ignoring the pain in this head, wrists, and ankles, he leapt up and charged Daria while she faced the other way, tackling her and slamming her down onto the floor without mercy. She screamed upon impact, and was stunned enough for him to wrench the gun out of her hands. "Sorry for making your bad day worse," Tony panted.

Daria was still screaming when McCully turned back and shouted, "You lying sonuvabitch! The light's not on!"

"Oh ... my mistake," Tony said, holding the gun on him. McCully reached again for his knife, but Tony fired a bullet into the floor, exactly between Rick's feet. "Drop it," he said. "I happen to be an excellent shot."

That was Tony Farland's second lie of the evening. He'd never held a gun before in his life. He'd been aiming at McCully's knee and missed.

But neither Rick McCully nor Daria Street knew that.

Three patrol cars arrived at the building in Hollywood before Detective Charleston showed up. By then, both Rick McCully and Daria Street were cuffed and in the back seat of their own cruisers. "Sorry I didn't get back to you, Mr. Farland," the detective said.

"It's okay," he replied. "In fact, it might have worked out better this way."

"Once you're through the emergency room, for that lump, I'll need you to come to the station and give a statement."

"I'll be delighted. Are you going to record it?"

"We'll take it down, sure. Why?"

"Oh, I'd kind of like to get a transcript if possible."

"What for?"

"I'm thinking of writing a book about this case," Tony said. "Since I like to be accurate, having a copy of my statement to you will certainly help."

"You've been beaten, tied up, and nearly murdered, and all you can think to do is write a book about it?"

"It will be of interest to film buffs. I'd be happy to send you a copy when it's out."

Charleston looked hard at Tony. "No offense, Mr. Farland," he said, "but I'd rather wait for the movie."

THE ILLUSION OF CONTROL

Josh Pachter

We step into the elevator, me and Mr. Rosetti, and he pushes the "Close Door" button like he does five days a week after leaving his office on the seventeenth floor of 44 Wall in the Financial District. Mondays through Thursdays, we head out on the dot of 5 PM, businessman's hours, but on Fridays we pick up the weekly payoffs from the dry cleaners and pizza joints and one-man shoe-repair shops and mom-and-pop groceries under our protection, and Mr. Rosetti likes to be home in Brooklyn in time to catch the six o'clock news, so on Fridays we head out at 3:30.

Today is Friday.

Usually, I keep my mouth shut when the boss hits that stupid button. This time, though, I'm pissed because of what he said about Pauline, my ex—who, yeah, she *is* a tramp, it's okay for me to say it but not nobody else, not even him. Even though we broke up, me and Pauline—which is to say she took up with another guy and kicked me out of the apartment we shared for the last four years—he's still got no right to go dissing her, I don't care *who* he is or *how* much muscle he's got behind him.

Comes to that, I *am* the muscle behind him, so this time I speak my mind for once. "You know that button don't do nothing," I say. "It's what you call a placebo."

"What are you talking about?" he frowns. "It closes the goddamn door, Gabe. *Look* at it. 'Close Door,' it says."

"Is the door closing?" I ask.

He makes a disgusted noise and jabs the button three more times, fast, one-two-three.

The door slides closed, and the elevator begins its descent.

"You see?" Mr. Rosetti says triumphantly. "Placebo, my ass."

I watch the illuminated numbers above the door blink from 15 to 14 to 12—more stupidstition, the idea that if you don't *call* the thirteenth floor the thirteenth floor, then the building ain't *got* no thirteenth floor—and I'm getting more bent out of shape by the second.

"The button don't make the door close no faster," I finally insist. "I read about it in a magazine the other day, while you were gettin' your teeth cleaned at Doc Mosher's. It's because of what you call the Americans With Disabilities Act, see? Elevator doors got to stay open long enough so people in wheelchairs can roll on in. You can push that button a hundred times, it won't—"

"I ask you for information, Alex Trebek?" he growls. "What are you, on *Jeopardy*?"

I grit my teeth. "It's like the crosswalk buttons," I say. "Ninety percent of them ain't even hooked up to nothin'. It's what you call the 'illusion of control,' you see what I mean? They want you to *think* you're in charge of stuff, even though the fact is you ain't. It's what you call psychology, is what it—"

"Shut the fuck up, Gabe," Mr. Rosetti spits. "I pay you to guard my body, not for psychology lessons. I want psychology, I'll call that Fraud guy."

I take a breath. "It's *Freud,*" I tell him. "Sigmund Freud. And he died like a hundred—"

"Shut. The fuck. Up. Gabriel." His eyes are flaming now. "I don't want to hear one more word out of your fuckin' mouth."

Well, Mr. Rosetti's the guy pays me, right, so I shut my fuckin' mouth—but it ain't so easy to shut off my brain, you know? Listen, he don't always treat me like dirt. He even give me a sharp pair of cufflinks my last birthday. They were his, I seen him wear them lots of times, I figure he must of just got tired of them, but still, he didn't have to give me nothing. That was a nice what you call gesture.

But still. He thinks because he's high up on the food chain he can say whatever he wants. Me, I'm just a foot soldier, it don't matter if I got feelings or whatever. I'm a pair of biceps and a gun to him, that's all. And tell you the truth, I'm getting pretty fuckin' tired of it.

The elevator settles to a stop on L, and the door slides open. I lean out and look both ways to make sure the coast is clear. At Mr. Rosetti's level in the Organization, he has enemies who would love to take over his share of the rackets, and my job is to take care of him.

The coast is clear, not a soul in sight.

So I lean back into the elevator and plug him, right in the middle of the forehead. That's enough right there to put him down, but just to make sure I give him another one in the pump.

I guess this means I'm through in New York, but now that Pauline and me are history I got nothing else tying me to the Big Apple. Before I take off and start looking for another gig in another town, I wrap my handkerchief around my hand and lean in and thumb the "Close Door" button.

It won't make the door close no faster, I know that.

But still, I like the way it makes me feel.

SPEAK OF THE DEVIL

Jeanne DuBois

Vera squeezed the last container of red velvet cake into the cooler and closed the lid. "I think that's everything."

Ashley, one of Vera's fourteen-year-old granddaughters, wheeled the cooler down the ramp into the garage and levered it into the sedan's trunk. Her twin was usually at hand, but this morning, the first Saturday of their spring break, Hannah was already up the street at Miss Betty's. Which sparked a little Q and A in the car.

"It wasn't dark when Hannah left, was it?"

"No, Mimi."

"Why couldn't she wait for us? There's a lot of traffic in the morning."

"She wanted to help Miss Betty get ready."

"There's no sidewalk there. You sure the sun was up?"

"There's a sidewalk on the other side, Mimi, and yes, the sun was up."

From a distance, the white-haired woman in the little veiled hat and floral shirtwaist appeared much younger than her ninety-one years. The shoes were a dead giveaway though. Sturdy black oxfords with Cuban heels, straight from the Forties. A matching snap-clasp handbag hung over her wrist. While Miss Betty climbed into the front seat, Hannah stowed a vintage green tote in the trunk, slid into the back with Ashley, and stretched out her everyday prosthetic with its matching tennis shoe and lifelike cover. Vera knew the cover was for her benefit. For school, Hannah wore one resembling black lace or no cover at all. Both girls had on skirts with shorts underneath. Hannah's skirt was yellow, Ashley's pink.

The drive from St. Augustine to Gainesville usually took around two hours, but today Vera planned to stop at Miss Betty's country house on the way. Curtis Brown, a distant cousin of Miss Betty's in his sixties, was supposed to be taking care of her country house in exchange for free rent and utilities. After repeated calls to the landline went unanswered, a friend's daughter drove by and reported a padlocked gate, waist-high weeds, and a ton of downed trees. Before Miss Betty worked herself into a state, Vera suggested she join them for a weekend of museums and softball, and see for herself.

Miss Betty looked out her window now and grumbled, "Curtis is probably fishing in the Keys. He's got an ex-brother-in-law in Marathon. Never could count on that side of the family. One of the nephews is a real piece of work. Killer Kenny, they call him. One time—"

"How long has Curtis lived there?" Vera didn't want to hear any more about Killer Kenny. Miss Betty's family stories verged on horror tales at times.

"Close on twenty years, I reckon."

Vera smiled to herself. "If he's moved, you shouldn't have any trouble finding somebody else to live there and take care of the place. I bet one of the neighbors can suggest someone." The traffic was heavy, as usual. Though most of the cars were heading toward the ocean, not away from it, as they were.

"There's no air conditioning," Miss Betty said. "You know how people are these days."

"Make them an offer they can't refuse," Vera said. "Like you did with Curtis."

"Uh huh."

"Can't you install some window units?" Ashley said.

"Wiring might not be up to the challenge, Ash," Vera said. "It's an old house. Your father built it, didn't he, Miss Betty?"

"Helped. He was still a kid in 1913. The wiring's not that old, of course. Place was remodeled in the Fifties. Still, Curtis had a devil of a time hooking up his fish freezer."

Ashley said, "Maybe you could sell the place."

"Oh, I can't do that," Miss Betty said.

"Why not?" Vera said. "The land itself must be worth a pretty penny, all the development going on everywhere these days."

"There's graves in the back."

Hannah turned to her twin. "Ooo, graves."

"Don't start," Ashley said.

Vera glanced sideways. "Like a family cemetery?"

Miss Betty's eyes shone. "Daddy's family. There's even an angel."

"We're here." Vera drove through an open farm gate in the middle of nowhere. So much for neighbors.

Apart from a few scattered limbs, the front yard didn't look that bad. The grass maybe needed a mow, but not like it would in June or July. Spikes of purple wildflowers poked up all over. Huge azalea bushes in front of the yellow cottage bloomed lavender pink. Leaves trickled down from a granddaddy oak on the right. The lime rock driveway, bumpy and potholed, was lined with sabal palms. Old ones, their trunks silver in the sun.

And then Vera spotted the men. Two of them. Armed with shovels. Digging at the base of one of the palms. Parked nearby was a dusty pickup hooked to a flatbed trailer with one tree laid out lengthwise, its root ball wrapped in black plastic, fronds trimmed and tied.

Vera slowed.

Miss Betty opened her eyes and twisted in her seat. "What are they doing?"

"They're stealing your trees," Hannah said.

"Stay in the car," Vera said, hearing Hannah's door unlatch, "until we sort things out."

But Hannah and Miss Betty were already in the driveway, stuck together like two peas in a pod, fast-walking toward the men. Vera jammed the car into park and hurried after them.

"My name is Betty Hughes and they're my trees," Miss Betty was saying when Vera caught up to them.

The older man was insistent. "I buy them from the owner." Unlike his bareheaded companion, who might have been his son, the man wore a hat woven from palm fronds. The boy had a red bandana tied around his neck. Both wore long-sleeved buttoned shirts with faded jeans and work boots.

"I'm the owner," Miss Betty said.

The man turned dark eyes on Vera.

Vera said, "Maybe your cousin sold them the trees."

Miss Betty looked toward the house. "Where is Curtis?"

"Not here." The man waved the boy toward the truck.

The boy was giving a dirt-stained paper to the hatted man when Ashley came to stand beside Vera. The man's calloused hand trembled slightly as he turned the paper over to Miss Betty.

Miss Betty showed it to Hannah. "I don't have my glasses. What's it say?"

"It says he paid five hundred dollars for ten trees."

"Curtis signed it?"

Hannah shrugged. "I guess."

Vera reached for the paper. “Somebody signed. Looks like initials. I can’t tell what they are either. Could be CB. Two days ago.”

“Had to be Curtis. He’s the only one living here.” Miss Betty took the receipt from Vera and handed it back to the man. “I think you already got some.” She jerked her thumb sideways. They all turned to look at the four tamped-down circles of dirt, except for the boy who walked back to the truck to replace the receipt on the dash. Fill dirt made a yellowish mound beyond the vehicle.

Miss Betty went on, “I’m not going to make you put the one you stole today back in the ground. Lucky for me, you took trees from both sides of the driveway.”

The man raised his arms. “I do not steal. I pay the owner.”

Miss Betty said, “Like I said, I’m the owner. Now,” she reached into her handbag and removed a checkbook, “I’ll write you a check for the—”

The man waved a hand. “No check.”

Miss Betty frowned. “I only have two twenties.”

“I have some cash,” Vera said. “Not close to two-sixty, though.”

Miss Betty returned the checkbook to her handbag. “I’ll have to get the money from Curtis.”

The man stared at his paper. “I buy ten.”

“I know what it says there. You want to call the Sheriff, be my guest, but you’re not digging up any more of my palms.” Miss Betty looked at the open gate. “Curtis give you a key to the padlock?”

The man had been shaking his head since Miss Betty said the word sheriff. “No key.”

“He’ll be back today?”

“Yes, he tell me leave open the gate.”

Miss Betty smiled. “Then we’ll see you later.”

The boy retrieved the shovels and dropped them in the bed of the pickup. The man checked the ropes on the palm. Neither of them made eye contact with the group gathered on the driveway as the truck and trailer exited the property.

Hannah said, “What’s to stop him from coming back for the rest of the trees after we leave?”

“Nothing,” Miss Betty said. “That’s why I’m going to wait here for Curtis. If he doesn’t have the cash to repay the man, I’ll make him take me to the nearest ATM.”

“I’m not leaving you here by yourself,” Vera said.

“We can all wait,” Hannah said, taking Miss Betty by the hand.

Instead of eating lunch outside the Florida Museum following a visit to the Butterfly Rainforest, they picnicked on the front porch of the yellow cottage and listened to the birds. There was an empty feeder near the satellite dish and Hannah decided they were all saying, in bird, "Hurry up and feed us, hurry up, hurry up and feed us."

"There's plenty of bugs and berries for them to eat around here," Vera said.

Hannah said, "But they want sunflower seeds and peanuts." As if to support her claim, a female cardinal landed atop the feeder with a chirp.

"Sorry," Vera said, "I didn't pack any bird food."

"Poor," Ashley said, sneezing in between the words, "birdies."

Miss Betty offered her a tissue from a travel pack in her lap and a dose of Benadryl from the new bottle in her handbag, which she asked Hannah to open for her.

Vera glimpsed a silver flask in Miss Betty's handbag and looked away, amused. What else did she have in there? So far, she'd pulled out a checkbook, hand sanitizer, sugar packets, paper straws, toothpicks, mints, eye drops, a mirrored compact, lipstick, tissues, and now allergy medicine.

"It's pretty here," Hannah said, handing back the bottle.

Planted pines stretched out forever across the road. The sky above was a wash of blue. White curtains hid the details of the house's interior, though the faint whomp-whomp of a ceiling fan was audible through the screened window.

Ashley blew her nose. "Except for all the tree pollen."

"Wait, Miss Betty," Vera said, "don't give her that. I have some non-drowsy stuff in my bag. I'll get it."

"What's wrong with mine? I got a clean medicine cup if that's what you're worried about." But Vera was already halfway to her car, parked in the shade of the old oak.

Vera returned with a foil-wrapped tablet. "We don't want her falling asleep on us."

"I might anyway," Ashley said.

"Me too," Hannah said. "Let's get up and do something."

"Like what?"

"Can we put flowers on the graves?"

Miss Betty clapped her hands. "What a lovely idea. Y'all go. I'll wait here for Curtis."

Vera looked doubtful. "I don't know." Hannah's prosthetic was designed for walking on mostly even terrain.

"There's a path," Miss Betty said, pointing opposite the oak.

"We'll go slow," Hannah promised.

Two years since her transfemoral amputation and Hannah was doing great. Way better than Vera. The physical therapist suggested Vera leave it to Hannah to decide what she could and couldn't do. What he didn't understand was that Hannah thought she could do everything. Vera was trying. When Hannah asked if she could get a running leg, Vera's first response was to shout, "No! Running is dangerous!" She'd come around in the end though. Hannah's sports prosthetic would be ready next Thursday.

After examining what she could see of the path, which appeared more like a narrow lime rock road than an overgrown nature trail, Vera gave permission for the girls to go it alone, even offered up two reusable shopping bags for the flowers. Miss Betty gave them one of the containers of red velvet cake, for sustenance on their walk, two juice boxes, and a handful of paper napkins from the depths of her handbag.

When the girls were out of sight, Miss Betty turned to Vera. "Ready for a look inside the house?"

"I thought you wanted to wait for Curtis."

Miss Betty batted her eyelashes at Vera. "I've never been one for peeing in the bushes."

Vera blushed. She'd made a quick trip while the others settled on the porch, camouflaged by the car. Or so she thought. "Should I be worried about bugs?" Palmettos were her nemesis. The large roaches liked to hole up in old buildings, flying around, sometimes, when disturbed.

"I don't think so," Miss Betty said. "Curtis was a Merchant Marine. He's always been a neat and tidy man."

But one step inside gave lie to that claim. Empty bottles of all colors littered the heart pine floor.

"Liquor bottles," Miss Betty said, kicking aside a clear one. "So, he's following that path now. Explains him selling the trees."

Something dark moved across the floor at the edge of Vera's vision.

"The males in that family always had a weakness for alcohol." Miss Betty walked on, oblivious to Vera freaking out behind her. "I never knew Curtis to drink. But people change."

Vera followed her down a hall and past two closed doors to the bathroom off a kitchen which was, not surprisingly, a complete disaster. Dirty dishes filled a farmhouse sink and covered its porcelain drainboard. The battered red Formica table was home to more bottles. A metal trash can in the corner overflowed with packaged meal remains.

Vera escaped through the back door. “I’ll wait outside.”

A few minutes later, Miss Betty joined Vera in the backyard, rubbing sanitizer over her hands. “I’m so disappointed. I’d rather he ran away to the Keys without telling me than be here drinking himself to death.” And then, “What’s that smell?”

Vera took a not-so-wild guess. “The kitchen?”

“No, it’s not that.”

Miss Betty headed for a barn-like building joined to the house by an orange extension cord. Vera followed. A few scraps of torn white paper littered the ground. Many more were scattered across the side yard under one long arm of the oak, visible as they rounded the building.

Vera picked one up. “There’s writing. ‘R E D F I.’ Redfish?”

“Did raccoons raid the freezer?” Miss Betty opened a door in the building’s back wall and went inside.

Light filtered through cracks in the vertical planks of the partition wall, painting everything with stripes. A chest freezer sat in the corner nearest the house. Vera placed her hand on its lid and felt a slight vibration.

“It’s on now,” she said. “Maybe there was a power outage.”

“Why didn’t he leave the fish inside to refreeze?”

“Maybe he took out the packages that thawed, but raccoons got into them before he could put out the trash.”

“You don’t ‘put out’ trash here,” Miss Betty said. “He’d have loaded the can into his truck and taken it to the dump.”

“When he was sober.”

“There is that.”

Vera opened the freezer. Its interior light flashed on. A human face, frozen in terror, greeted them. The man’s body lay bent and contorted, arms outstretched. The women grabbed each other, jumping and screaming. After a few seconds, Vera freed herself and slammed the lid.

Miss Betty fumbled in her handbag, then handed Vera the silver flask. “It’s Curtis.”

The sweet liquor burned, all the way down, sending a wave of warmth throughout her body. It was Miss Betty’s turn next. She sipped and coughed, sipped and coughed, sipped and coughed. Vera had no words. Curtis was obviously alive when he went in the freezer. There were scratch marks on the inside of the lid.

Who would do such a thing? Not the palm tree man. No need for a receipt if the owner were dead. Unless Curtis sobered up and changed his mind. Still, it seemed an unlikely reaction to missing out on a few palms. On the other hand, if the palm tree man charged the normal three hundred fifty dollars for each mature tree he installed, he stood to make three thousand dollars on the deal.

"I have to get the girls," Vera said, heading for the door.

Miss Betty said, "Text them."

"All our phones are in the car." Vera regretted her strict adherence to the no-screens-during-mealtime rule. "I'll be quick." She stepped outside.

A huge arm closed around Vera's neck before she could scream. It reeked of alcohol and sweat. Vera kicked and scratched and tried to bite. The man's belly vibrated against her back. He was laughing. And then he wasn't. He tossed Vera aside. Miss Betty was beating him with a broom handle.

The broom head, a long bristly affair for sweeping out garages, lay by the door. Vera kicked it out of her way, ran in the shed, and came out with an extension cord. The giant was holding the broom handle aloft while Miss Betty gave him hell with her old-timey shoes. He watched her, enthralled. Like she was the eighth wonder of the world. Vera lassoed him with a loose loop of cord from behind. And then another. And now there were three. He seemed not to mind. Until Vera put her weight on the loops hanging down his back. Then he quickly dropped the broom to paw at his neck. Miss Betty retrieved it in a flash and smacked him a few times between the legs. He collapsed, finally, with a moan.

"And that's how they caught the wooly mammoths," Vera said, coiling the extension cord around him as he writhed on the ground, hands like softball gloves protecting his privates. A foot-and-a-half taller than Miss Betty and at least a yard wider, he had a mop of graying hair, a bad case of razor burn, and red-rimmed eyes. His paint-stained work shirt was big as a tent.

While Miss Betty ministered to the big man with her flask and medicine bottle, streaming small amounts of the liquids into his open mouth from afar, like a living fountain, Vera searched the shed for another cord or a rope. When she emerged empty-handed, the man lay in the sun, swaddled in yellow extension cord, eyes closed, smiling contentedly. Miss Betty turned the flask and Benadryl bottle upside down for Vera with a wink. Both were empty.

"Yo!" An angry voice split the silence. "Gus!"

To their dismay, the big man broke free of the yellow cord without much effort and staggered to his feet. "Huh?"

This new man was smaller and younger than Vera, but not by much. Filthy jeans, a stretched-out T-shirt, straggly hair, dirty beard. The usual suspects.

“Speak of the devil,” Miss Betty said, crossing her arms.

The new man regarded her with exaggerated disbelief. “Betty? How are you even still alive?”

“Hello, Kenny.”

The man laughed. “You don’t sound happy to see me. Now why is that? Did you find Uncle Curtis, by any chance?”

Miss Betty didn’t answer. She was backing away and pulling Vera along with her.

“Oh no you don’t,” Kenny said. “Stand right where you are. Gus, toss me that extension cord. Punch ’em both in the head either one moves.”

Vera froze. One punch from that fist and they’d both be history.

Kenny chatted as he wrapped the cord tightly around Vera’s midsection. “I ran into my tree guy at the gas station. He says an old lady won’t let him get the trees I sold him and he wants his money back. I says, ‘Hey, a deal’s a deal, they’re your trees.’ He says, “She’s not the owner?’ I says, ‘No, I told you before, my first name’s Kenny, and my last one’s Brown, like it says on the mailbox.’ Then I says, ‘The old biddy won’t be around tomorrow,’ and he says, ‘Okay, see you in the morning.’ So I got ’til then to get things tied up around here. If you know what I mean.”

Vera’s heart sank.

Kenny led their little parade through the dark woods, ripping spider webs apart with the broom handle. Vera was second, her arms trapped by coils of extension cord. Miss Betty, tied to Vera with the same cord, was a-little-too-close third. Gus brought up the rear, a quiet goer for all his bulk. They were headed for the grave already dug for Curtis in the family cemetery. Big enough for two, Kenny said. Vera consoled herself with this, figuring it meant Kenny didn’t know about the twins.

Vera stomped twigs and dry leaves, trying to make as much noise as possible along the way. Yelling a warning would only alert the men to the girls’ existence, one of whom couldn’t outrun a gopher tortoise. And whose fault was that, Vera? A wave of guilt crashed onto her shoulders, causing her to stumble. Small hands touched Vera’s back and side, helping her regain her balance. Vera carried on, eyes-wide. Miss Betty’s hands were free.

After ten minutes, or a week, the leaf-covered ground gave way to a carpet of pine needles and the canopy opened up. Hannah’s accident was replaying itself over and over in Vera’s mind. The phone call. The bloody scene. The oh-so-sorry driver who hit Hannah’s bike in the pedestrian crosswalk. The hospital. The emergency amputation.

Two years later, the images and the feelings they evoked were sharp as broken glass.

Vera shook her head to stop the video. Time to quit distracting herself with the pain and face the reality. She was being marched to her death.

Miss Betty called out, “Hey, Kenny, you remember Aunt Maisie, don’t you?”

Kenny kept walking.

“I take that as a yes.” Miss Betty’s southern accent intensified as her voice grew louder. “Aunt Maisie was the only one could keep you from misbehavin’ at our last family reunion here. You remember that? You were about twelve, I reckon. Aunt Maisie musta whipped your butt thirty times that day. Guess she didn’t like the way you were treatin’ her animals.”

He tossed a quick “shut up” over his shoulder.

“Funny thing, Kenny,” Miss Betty was practically shouting now, “after y’all went home, we found bug poison in her sugar bowl. White, just like sugar, but with little specks of blue and green and orange in it. Imagine that.”

Kenny’s head turned, eyes blazing. “I told you to shut up.”

“Just making conversation.”

Vera sent Miss Betty a silent thanks. Surely her words would carry and warn the girls.

“Everybody knew how sweet Aunt Maisie liked her tea,” Miss Betty went on. “She’s buried up ahead. Some folks say her spirit walks whenever she gets mad. Hope she’s not still mad about that bug poison in her sug—”

Kenny wheeled around, swinging the broom handle. Vera ducked. Miss Betty squeaked. A grunt from Gus. Vera glanced up. Gus was holding the other end of the wooden staff away from their heads.

“You’re right,” Kenny said, jerking it free, “if I knock them out here, you’ll have to carry them.”

Kenny sneered at Vera and told her to get going. She shivered. But maybe it was Miss Betty’s touch on her back. The cords seemed to be loosening. Vera could wriggle her arms a little. And take a deep breath.

Layers of pine straw muffled their footsteps now. No handy twigs to break. No dry leaves. Only some large pinecones that silently sank into the straw when she stepped on them. Vera spotted the weathered statue first. Draped in robes, bugle at the ready, the short-haired angel stood watch. Vera scanned the area for a glimpse of the girls and saw nothing. No lavender pink azalea blossoms. No pink or yellow skirt. No orange reusable shopping bags. Only a lone deer staring back from its hiding place in a different wood.

There was no iron fence. Upright headstones, worn by the years, blended in with dappled shade. Once Vera saw one, the others appeared as if by magic, rooted in pine straw, streaked with gray and black and the darkest green. They were everywhere. An eerie silence pounded in Vera's ears. Mounds of grayish sand marked the newest grave. Kenny pushed Vera toward it. Miss Betty's feet got tangled up with hers. Gus laid a steadying paw on Vera's shoulder. She felt the cords shift. She could move her elbows a few inches away from her body now.

Kenny planted the broom handle in a pile of sandy soil and strode around the mounds. "Where's the shovel? I thought I told you to leave the shovel. We need the shovel. Where'd you put the shovel, Gus?"

Gus lumbered past Vera and peered down into the hole.

Kenny said, "So, what now? We push them in and kick dirt on top of them? It's a plan. Not the one I—"

Movement in the cemetery caused them all to look. A body was rising up from the pine straw piled in front of the angel. Its face was gray. Reddish goo leaked from its mouth. A scream died on Vera's lips. The zombie's skirt might have been gray now, but it had been yellow when they started on this trip a few hours ago. The zombie began to moan. Vera's head felt like it was going to explode.

While Vera thrashed about within the confines of the wrapped cord, moving her feet ineffectually forward, Miss Betty was pulling backward with a strength Vera didn't know the elderly woman possessed. There was a loud thump.

Kenny twisted around. "Gus?"

An insistent moan made Kenny turn his attention back to the zombie. Red goo dripped from its chin now. Kenny stood frozen, mouth agape. Vera tried to force the coils downward so she could step out of them, but Miss Betty seemed determined to lift them over their heads. The pair teetered on the edge of the grave, pulling the tangled extension cord in opposite directions. Kenny leaped for the broom handle. He swung it at the zombie. Vera's heart stopped.

The broom handle connected with the zombie's raised right leg. The crack echoed around the cemetery. Both went flying. The severed leg landed among the pine needles, a tennis shoe still on its foot. There was no blood anywhere. The zombie kept coming. On one leg.

Kenny dropped to his knees, screaming, "No! Don't eat me! I'm sorry! I'm sorry about the bug poison! I'm sorry! Don't eat me!"

That's what Ashley and the sheriff's deputy heard when they jumped out of his cruiser at the end of the lime rock path.

Hannah was seated on the ground, wiping half-chewed red velvet cake and dirt off her face onto the underside of her T-shirt, while the deputy took care of Killer Kenny and the drowsy giant lying at the bottom of the newest grave. "Excellent timing, Ash. I can only hop so far."

Ashley's face was almost as gray as Hannah's when she handed over the prosthetic and pulled Hannah to her foot. "You said you were going to hide."

"Don't fret. I meant it to come off," Hannah said, reattaching her everyday leg. "I thought I might need to hit someone with it." The cover was cracked. But the rest looked good as new. "People are always afraid of prosthetic limbs for some reason. Even you, right, Mimi?"

"We can't decide," Vera rumbled, "which one of us gets to yell at you first. What were you thinking! You could have been killed! I can't believe you thought that was a good idea! Even though you probably saved our lives," Vera added with a rush of emotion and a hug.

"Guess that means you're up next." Hannah's arms encircled Miss Betty, who'd started to cry.

Vera held onto Ashley for a long minute. "You saved the day. How d'you know to call 9-1-1?"

"The birds stopped singing," Ashley said, "and I ran to the house to find out what was happening. But I never called 9-1-1. Hannah's and my cell phones were smashed and yours was dead on the dash. By the time I figured out how to use that weird phone in the house, the deputy was pulling in the driveway. He said some man called for a wellness check on his mother."

Miss Betty and Vera exchanged puzzled looks. Neither of them had a son. Or a son-in-law. Not one living, anyway.

A few weeks later, Vera was putting clean sheets away in the linen closet when Hannah jogged behind her with the news. "Miss Betty's back."

Hannah's sports prosthetic didn't even pretend to be human. The foot looked like something you'd see on a giant sewing machine. Or an alien. Hannah didn't mind. She thought it was wonderful. Said her new leg felt like a pillow on her stump. Vera'd replied, "I'm so glad your stump is comfy," which was a first. That Vera could say the word stump without blubbering shocked all three of them; Ashley almost fell out of her chair.

Hannah jogged around her bedroom and back down the hall, shrugging into a reflective vest. "Mr. Brown's ashes are on their way to the Keys."

“Mr. Brown?” Vera closed the door to the linen closet. “Oh, Curtis.”

Hannah jogged around the dim kitchen. “Miss Betty found someone to caretake her country house.”

Vera walked down the hall and turned on the light. “Who?”

Hannah was heading out the porch door into the dusky evening. She said something over her shoulder as the door slammed.

Vera made a face. “Lagonda Table? Never heard of her.”

Her gaze shifted to the dining table. On a beach-themed runner stood the usual glass vase of flowers. Mixed in with today’s gerbera daisies were several roses woven from palm fronds. Ah, Vera thought, the palm tree man. Miss Betty’s surprising “son.”

THE IMPATIENT INMATE

Michael Scherer

I focused on the top of the wall surrounding the prison yard. Razor wire reflected the morning sun and created row upon row of sparkling diamond tiaras. A mix of aromas vented from the prison kitchen—bacon and freshly brewed coffee—and the damp, bleach-clean scent of the laundry saturated the morning air. Odd, but familiar.

Across the prison yard a soft, twisted puff of air kicked up a dust devil, and I found myself lost in the wonder. How could something as soft and gentle as a kiss on the cheek create chaos where none existed before?

I love mornings. A perfect time to ponder life's little mysteries. The peace. The serenity. The quiet. The—

"Stoney. Tell this little shit to help me out."

So much for peace and quiet.

I shielded my eyes, peered across the yard at Hawk. Chuck Duncan was his real name. A twitchy son of a bitch always on the lookout for intrigue and conspiracies where none existed. Look up the word paranoid in the dictionary, and you'll find Hawk's picture. Hawk was arguing with Cliff McNett, a young Robert Redford type.

I stood, slogged across the dusty prison yard, reached the bickering couple then asked, "What is it?"

"Cliff won't hook me up with that classic Vette I want."

"Be real, Hawk. Cliff's been in the joint for six years. He doesn't *have* connections anymore.»

"Bullshit! He stole twelve vintage Vettes in eight days. Cliff's a living legend," Hawk said. "Like me."

Cliff spat on the ground. "Tell you what I'll do, Hawk. Tell me where you stashed that twenty-million from the armored car robbery and my associates will take just enough to get you that Vette."

"You're a punk, Cliff." Hawk backed away. "You're all punks. You all want my money. *My money*. Screw you all." Hawk stormed off.

I faced Cliff. "He ain't gonna be worth a shit the rest of the day. You know that, right?"

Cliff shrugged. "Money ain't doin' him no good. He has what, six years left?"

"Five."

"Whatever. You know how to handle money." Cliff inched closer, lowered his voice. "Get him to tell you where the money is. Get him to ask for some financial advice. I mean, you can't just waltz into a bank and open an account with that kind of dough."

I shook my head. "Hawk's right. This money thing has you tied up in knots." I looked left where Caleb Hunter, the youngest inmate in this joint, sat against a fence reading. The Kid always had his nose in a book. Kept to himself. Kept quiet. Barely spoke ten words all day. I turned back to Cliff. "You should be more like the Kid over there and mind your own business."

"Com'on, Stoney."

"Look, the last person I helped with financial advice turned State's evidence. He got witness protection. I got twenty years. No thanks."

Cliff sat on his haunches and drew dollar signs in the dirt. He looked over at the Kid and yelled, "Hey, Hunter? You know where Hawk's money is?"

Without looking up, the Kid shrugged, shook his head, continued reading.

Cliff stood. "You'd think Hunter would know being Hawk's cellmate for almost two years."

"Hawk wouldn't tell his own mother where the money was if her life depended on it." I stretched and rolled my neck. Vertebrae cracked like a string of firecrackers. It felt good, and I relaxed. "Face it. When Hawk gets out, he'll be one rich ex-con."

Cliff slapped me on the back. "Can't blame a guy for trying. It is a helluva lot of money." He laughed and shuffled off.

I strolled over to the Kid, stopped and cast a long shadow over him and his book. I liked the Kid. Kept his nose clean, minded his own business. He was in for a simple B&E and was due for release in two weeks. I'll miss him.

The Kid closed his book and looked up. "Whazzup?"

"Do me a solid?" I asked.

"Sure."

"Bring me an extra paper from work." The Kid was on work release at the local paper. His uncle was a big shot there. An editor I think.

Mischief danced in his eyes, or was it the Sun?

"OK."

The next morning all hell broke loose in Hawk's cell.

The man had gone ape-shit. Guards in riot gear had rushed into his cell, pulled the Kid to safety and subdued Hawk with a Taser.

After the dust had settled and things calmed down, I went to the Kid's cell, stepped inside and asked, "What the hell happened?"

He looked up. He sported a shiner and a small bruise on his cheek but otherwise seemed okay.

"Hawk do that?"

He nodded then smiled. He reached under his pillow, handed me my newspaper.

I stuck it in my back pocket.

He slipped off his bunk, stared at me and said, "Read it."

"Later."

"Now." He pulled the paper out of my pocket, handed it back. "Please."

I unfolded the newspaper, stared at the front page. The headline read: *Feds Locate Missing Money From '01 Armored Car Heist.*

"Holy shit!"

The Kid laughed. Deep and loud.

I had to admit the whole thing was ironic. I laughed too.

The Kid settled down and strung more words together at one time than I had ever heard him utter at one time.

"The headline's phony."

"What?"

"My uncle made it up for me. You know, like they do at carnivals or the state fair?"

"You mean—"

"I wanted to pull that moron's chain before I got out of here."

"You little prick. Does Hawk know?"

"He should, by now."

"Oh, man. He's gonna to make your life so miserable."

"He's harmless."

"He's nuts. Watch your back."

That afternoon I saw trouble rocket across the prison yard like a heat-seeking missile. Hawk made a beeline straight for the Kid.

I raced to intercept Hawk but was two steps too late.

He pounced on the Kid and bitch-slapped him several times.

I grabbed Hawk by the hair and yanked him to the ground. "Go," I ordered the Kid. "You don't need trouble. Not now. Not with two weeks left."

He picked up his book, dusted it off, and retreated across the yard.

I waited for him to reach the other side. When he squatted in the shade of the prison laundry, I sat Hawk down on the bench.

He kept his eyes on the Kid and the veins in his neck pulsed with every heartbeat. His blood pressure must have been sky-high. He stood and stared across the yard.

I pushed him down and said, "Talk to me, Hawk."

"Lil' bastard." He tried to stand again.

I pushed him back. "It was a joke, Hawk."

"Lil' bastard."

"Come on, you have to admit, it was pretty damn funny."

Hawk shot me a look. Anger flooded his eyes. If looks could kill.

"OK. Maybe not to you. But look at the bright side."

Hawk frowned then said, "What bright side?"

"The Kid's gone in two weeks."

The throbbing in his neck disappeared, and his shoulders relaxed. He nodded then looked past me. The blood drained from his face, and Hawk settled into a thousand-yard, deer-in-the-headlights, stiff-as-a-board stare.

I followed his gaze. The warden's assistant, Schwartz, stormed straight for us.

"Shit. They're going to throw me in solitary," Hawk said.

"Nah. They would have done that this morning," I said, more for my benefit than Hawk's.

Schwartz arrived, bent over and grabbed his knees. He huffed and puffed and wheezed and after several seconds, stood straight. He nodded at me, then wiped beads of sweat from his brow, and gasped again before setting his gaze on Hawk. Schwartz displayed a severe look on his ugly puss.

"Warden wants to see you, Hawk. Now."

Hawk's eyes locked on mine and his expression pleaded for some kind of help.

I shrugged, patted him on the back, and watched him leave.

No one spoke at dinner. Hawk's chair sat empty. I think we all had visions of him locked in solitary eating bread and water. The Kid took it the hardest. He sat there with his head down, pushing his food from one side of his plate to the other in complete silence. He looked terrible.

And then, there he was.

Hawk.

Free as a bird.

He carried a dinner tray and grinned like the village idiot. He stopped at our table, nodded at an empty chair. "You gents save me a seat?"

The Kid looked up. His expression went from somber to silly, and I half expected him to leap out of his chair and kiss Hawk.

The Kid pointed to an empty seat next to him and said, "Sit. Please."

Ever the man of few words.

Hawk kept that grin on his face as he sat next to the Kid and attacked his dinner.

No one else ate. We all waited for an explanation.

And waited.

At long last Hawk dropped his fork, leaned back in his chair. His gaze swept over the table. "Gentlemen, you are looking at a free man."

Cliff stared at Hawk and said, "You get religion or something?"

"No, Mr. McNett. But I would like to place that order for a '60 Corvette convertible now."

I rolled my eyes. *Oh Christ, not this again?*

Hawk continued, "And, it must be Tasco turquoise." He looked up and down the table with that stupid look plastered across his face. He acted all antsy and excited, and I realized he was bursting at the seams to say what was really on his mind. He couldn't hold back any longer.

"I'm being released in three days. Time served and good behavior." He pumped a fist in the air. "A free man. A very, very rich, free man."

The Kid gagged on his meatloaf, took a long drink of water, recovered.

"So, Mr. McNett. Can you get me the Vette?"

"Three days?" Cliff asked. "My associates might arrange something. For a price."

"Money, my dear fellow, is no object," he said. "And stenciled on the rear quarter panel I want the words, *Thank$ A Million.*" He laughed, pleased with his good fortune and his wit.

I sat there utterly bewildered. It didn't fit. No lawyers? No negotiations? No parole hearing? Just, here's your hat, what's your hurry. It didn't ring true. "Hawk, I hate to rain on your parade, but there has to be a catch."

"No catch. Just good fortune."

"You walk? Just like that?"

"What can I say, Stoney, I lead a charmed life."

The Kid stood. He was green around the gills and looked ready to puke.

"Hey, Kid, you okay?" I asked.

"Gotta get to work," he mumbled. He looked like he just lost his best friend.

Hawk scooted his chair forward to give the Kid some room. "Hey, Hunter. Have your uncle print this, Charles Duncan, the world's newest millionaire." He laughed. Hard. The first time I'd ever heard Hawk laugh.

And the last.

Schwartz rousted Cliff and me out of bed an hour before morning wake-up, and he didn't look none too happy.

"Where's Hunter?"

"The Kid?" I looked at Cliff, he at me. I turned my attention back to Schwartz. "Check with Hawk."

"We did. Hunter ain't there, and he never checked back through the gate."

"Maybe he's still at work. Overtime or something."

"Checked that too. Hunter never showed up at work. Looks like he's skipped."

"With ten days left to serve? That would be pretty damn stupid. And the Kid ain't stupid." I sat on my bunk, cleared the cobwebs from my sleepy brain. "Maybe something happened to him on the way to work. You know it ain't safe on the outside."

Schwartz shook his head. "Don't think so. Hunter turned left outside the wall. We have it on tape. His workplace is to the right. Don't hold out on me, Stoney. Did he say anything about skipping out?"

I stood, ran my fingers across my scalp. "Nope. The Kid hardly speaks ten words all day. You know that."

"What about you, McNett? Anything?"

Cliff smiled. "Bet he went to get laid. Right, Stoney? You told him what he needed to loosen up was a good piece of—"

I cut Cliff off with a look. "He ain't out getting laid. Schwartz is right. The Kid skipped."

The next morning the Kid was back in his cell. Turned himself in. Claimed he got drunk, crawled into bed with some college sweetie, spent all night and half the day getting to know her. With that stupid grin on his face, I believed him. He was one happy camper. Nothing, not even the extra six months they tacked on his sentence, could wipe that grin off his face.

Hawk said his goodbyes the next day. He took great pleasure in letting the Kid know he thought he was an idiot for exchanging six months of his life for a girl he didn't even know. "Couldn't be worth it, Hunter. No broad is."

The Kid pawed the ground with his foot, grinned that stupid grin, never saying a word.

Two days later Hawk was back in his cell.

He wouldn't talk. Just sulked all day. Couldn't get a word out of him. I ended up bribing a clerk in the warden's office to sneak a peek at Hawk's file. Cost me three packs of smokes and worth every damn cancer stick.

Seems when Hawk left he headed straight for the money. Just what the Feds figured he would do. With cash in hand, they arrested him for violating his parole. Possession of stolen property, they said. It was a good plan. The Feds recover the bank's millions, and Hawk finishes his twenty-year sentence.

Only there were no millions. At least that's what Hawk told me when he finally opened up.

"Bastards set me up," Hawk said. "They took my fucking money and set me up."

"And if you could have waited two more days, the Statute of Limitations would have kicked in, and you would have been home free."

"Statue of what?"

"Statute of Limitations. In this state, after fifteen years, the money is no longer considered stolen. Legally, it's up for grabs. Anyone who finds the money can keep it. Free and clear."

"And the Feds knew that?"

"It's why they let you out early. To lead them to the money."

Hawk looked confused. He faced me. "But they already knew."

"Knew what?"

"Knew where the money was."

"How do you figure?"

He checked the area for eavesdroppers then whispered, "Between you, me and the prison walls?"

I nodded.

He leaned in close. “There was only a hundred grand. They already had my money.”

“Then why let you out?”

“Because they’re pricks.”

The next few months flew by. Hawk kept to himself and folks reciprocated. The Kid still grinned like an idiot. Maybe that girl really was worth the extra six months. Maybe he was in love. But, then again, maybe not. No one ever came to visit him. No girl. No family. No one. Not even his uncle.

The Kid’s release date arrived. He said his goodbyes in the prison yard. Cliff gave him a hug, whispered something in his ear and slipped him a piece of paper.

The Kid stepped up to Hawk, extended his hand.

Hawk hesitated before shaking the Kid’s hand. No words exchanged. No good luck. No goodbyes.

He got around to me last. Gave me a hug. I would have preferred a handshake. “Good luck, Kid,” I said.

“Yeah, you too.” He stared at Hawk and continued, “I’ll be sending you something in the mail.” He winked at me and smiled. “Keep a lookout for it.”

With that, he turned and walked out of our lives.

The Kid’s letter arrived last week. Inside there was a note, along with another envelope that felt like it contained photos. The note read: *Only open in the presence of Stoney, Cliff, and Hawk.*

I gathered everyone in the courtyard on a bright sunny morning. Dust devils floated above the ground, diamond tiaras danced along the fence. I told them what was up.

Cliff rubbed his hands together. “Bet it’s a picture of that girl he laid.”

“I’ll bet she’s a skank. A real bow-wow,” Hawk said.

I opened the envelope, removed one of the photos. It was the Kid. And a girl. A blonde, a real looker. There was another note. This one addressed to Hawk. I handed it to him.

Hawk unfolded the paper. “Probably an apology.” A troubled look crossed his face. He handed me the note. “What does this mean?”

I read the note aloud. “Hawk, for the record, you talk in your sleep. A lot.”

I shrugged. “Beats me.”

Cliff nudged me. “Let’s see the other photo.”

I pulled out the picture, Cliff whistled. “Wow. Just might be worth six months in the joint. What you think, Hawk? Was she worth it?”

Hawk leaned in to get a better look. He gulped, almost gagged, turned beet-red and looked ready to blow a gasket.

The Kid and the girl sat in a Tasco turquoise ’60 Corvette. Painted on the rear quarter panel: *Thank$ A Million, Hawk!*

Hawk turned and walked away.

REMOTE STORAGE

Susan Hammerman

People who turned up at the library were lost in the county court building, there to get a divorce, file a lawsuit, or at the express invitation of the police. The library was closed, had been for hours, and the door was locked. Someone banged on it a second time. John Connelly slapped his hand on his desk at the interruption. Whoever it was didn't want the library anyway.

Two more bangs were followed by a series of vigorous kicks that rattled the doorknob. It was a full-blown temper tantrum.

It didn't help to lean back in his desk chair. John couldn't see the four-foot-long glass panel in the door, not until he stood up, walked over, and got just about on top of it. And when he did, he saw two men. He knew one of them, but what he paid attention to was the baseball bat in the guy's hand. John dropped back and pressed himself against the wall next to the door, out of sight he hoped. A bat could smash the thin sheet of glass in the door with no problem. He wished he'd been wrong and amended that to he wished he'd stayed out of it.

The lights flickered, clicked, and the room went silent. He flipped the light switch off. That added dark to the quiet. John knew he had to get to the other side of the door. He dropped down and crawled as fast as a forty-three-year-old librarian with bad knees can. The window shattered. Sharp rain poured down on his head. He scrambled forward, jumped up, and wildly ran his hands up the wall. When his fingers found it, he yanked the fire alarm handle. It shrieked to life. Like bears, John thought, they would be scared away by the noise, but they were dumb bears and stayed put. From the light in the hallway, John saw a pork chop hand inch through the attached shards of glass in the window frame and reach for the doorknob and the lock.

Three Hours Earlier

The fluorescent lights buzzed like happy bumblebees lolling on daisies. As the seconds ticked by, the buzzing grew. The bees were joined by friends and then by enemies. The lights flickered twice, clicked, and went silent for fifty seconds. John Connelly's days fulfilling one pointless task after another as the librarian in the municipal records library were measured in audio segments from the ceiling lights.

More records had come in from the mosquito abatement department. They smelled vaguely of insecticide. Twenty stuffed manila folders were stacked on the library's wooden counter. John needed to put the pages in some kind of order, remove the staples that would rust and stain the paper, then box the records in grey archival boxes to ensure their preservation. First, he had to check if there was room on the library's metal shelves for the new records. If there wasn't, and he was pretty sure there wasn't, he would have to shift boxes to make room. All the mosquito abatement records, going back to 1971, were shelved together. No one had ever come in to use them.

Bored at the prospect, but with nothing better to do instead, John flipped up the short movable section in the wooden counter and walked through the narrow gap. He always thought it was stupid that he was protected from the public by a wooden counter that stretched the length of the room, and the records were sitting on the open shelves. Anyone could pull library material off a shelf and sit down at one of three large white tables and read it or walk off with it.

The spongy soles of his chukka boots squeaked on the yellow linoleum tiles as he crossed the room to the thirty aisles of shelving.

Before he was halfway down the aisle, he saw the shelves were jam-packed. Scanning in front of him, he tried to figure out the easiest way to shift the old boxes to make room for the new ones. There wasn't an easy way.

The metal bell on the counter pinged. John heard it clearly, because the lights were in the happy bee phase. He peered back down the aisle and saw two men standing at the counter. He retraced his steps. From the back of them, John knew they were in the wrong place. One guy was in a black leather coat, and the other was in a jean jacket and a baseball cap. They probably wanted the DMV, across the street.

"What can I do you for?" John asked their backs, as he flipped the section of counter up and squeezed through, putting him on the staff side of things.

When John got a look at their faces, he knew they were lost. Jean jacket had a sleazy mustache and a raging case of pink eye. Leather coat had sunglasses shoved up his forehead and a broken finger, which was strapped to his ring finger with grubby, white medical tape. He was drumming the three working fingers of his right hand on the counter as if it had taken John an age instead of seconds to greet them.

"Building plans. 1357 South Polk Street," pink eye said like he was ordering a beer.

"The old pumping station," the other one added.

John processed the fact that they were in the right place and said, "Okay, sure." He handed a form and a pencil to the guy without an eye infection. "Fill out this reader registration form, and I need to see your driver's license."

Technically, to request library materials, both of them should have shown him their IDs and filled out forms, listing their full names and addresses. But eye infections trumped the rules.

Leather jacket had trouble working the pencil. John worried that pink eye might take over for him, but he didn't. He just stood there with his hands jammed in his pockets.

The form was nearly legible when leather jacket pushed it back across the counter. His name turned out to be Vince Bauer.

"And your driver's license," John said.

"It might be expired," Vince said and opened his wallet.

John made another quick adjustment to the rules. The DMV was across the street, but if he asked Vince to renew his driver's license, then pink eye might produce his instead. John didn't want to handle his driver's license any more than he wanted to handle his registration form. He picked up Vince's license. It expired three years ago. He compared the address on the license to what Vince had written on the form. It matched.

"Take a seat, and I'll get the drawings. What's the address?" John asked.

"1357 South Polk," pink eye said.

"No pens, no photography," John said over the buzzing lights.

A little typing and a few clicks in the library's catalog brought up the box number and aisle number: six oversize, in aisle three. John crossed the room, found the four-foot-long box, and deposited it on the reading table where the two men were sitting. He pried off the lid. The drawings were face down. The addresses were written in pencil on the upper right corners of each page. He flicked through the pages until he found the drawings for 1357 South Polk. Carefully, he pulled the three large beige sheets from the box and flipped them over. The first drawing, rendered in graphite and ink, was of the building's brick façade and interior. It was dated 1889. The second page showed the pumping mechanism, and the third was of the tunnels that transported water and sewage.

John knew the building. It was by the river and hadn't operated as a pumping station in eons, not for at least sixty years or more. He'd helped amateur railroad buffs at the library plenty of times. These two were his first pumping station enthusiasts. There was no accounting for boring hobbies.

"Need anything else?" he asked, hoping they didn't.

"I can't take a picture with my phone?" Vince asked. "Even no flash?"

John shook his head no. "Sorry."

"What about copies?" Vince asked.

"It's too big. I can make a scan and forward the image to your email."

Tina from the mayor's office pushed a book truck loaded with archival boxes through the door. She had to lean into the truck to move it, which looked like a struggle in her high heels.

She parked the truck near the wall and hollered over the lights, "He's done with these."

John came over, so she could hear him. "The mayor had those records for two years."

"Three," she said. "He never looked at them once."

The lights flickered, clicked, and pink eye said, "Bank vault."

The lights were silent, and the two men went silent too. It was a tense awkward quiet, what might follow if pink eye had yelled out his mother's bra size at her funeral.

John turned around and was met with a double image of tough guy stares. There was no doubt that banks and vaults were none of his business. John turned back to Tina. She shrugged at the exchange and gave John a wave goodbye with her long fake turquoise fingernails.

The two men were back to studying the tunnels when John got behind the counter again.

Pink eye said to Vince, "Eddie?" He said it low, but the room was quiet.

"My son? No," Vince said. "What about your girlfriend?"

"Which one?" pink eye laughed.

"Yeah, right. Give it to him," Vince said, jerking his thumb towards John.

"I don't know it."

"Call her and ask her for it."

Pink eye pulled out his phone and dialed. "Hey, babe. It's me," he said. "I need your email." He paused. Then he cupped his hand over his mouth and said, "I just need it." He stood up and walked into the hall to continue his argument in private.

Vince turned up his hard guy routine a notch or two as John approached him.

John considered saying the scanner was broken, but he didn't think he could make that sound convincing and asked, "You want the scans? It's two dollars a page. All three pages?"

“Just this.” Vince poked at the tunnels.

John knew that would be the one he wanted. What were they planning? A bank robbery? He carried the drawing to the counter and laid it down.

Pink eye came back in, rested an elbow on the counter, and said, “Okay.”

Through the phone John heard a woman’s voice. “Patty362436 at AOL.”

John grabbed a piece of paper, scribbled it down, and spelled, “P-a-t-t-y?”

“One t,” the woman said. “362436 at AOL.”

Pink eye clicked a button to end the call.

John wanted them out of the library. He moved further back behind the counter, and positioned the drawing on the flatbed scanner, and scanned the image.

He sent the email to Paty with one t and on an impulse forwarded a copy of the scan to his personal email too. He charged Vince two dollars, and they left without revealing anything else about their plans.

As John was coming back from reshelving the box, he heard the phone ring and had to sprint to the desk to answer it.

“What did Randy want? What’s he up to?” She didn’t identify herself, but John knew that it could only be Paty on the line.

This time, he would not bend the rules and said, “It’s the library’s policy not to disclose that information.”

“Why?” she asked and then said to someone in the room with her, “He won’t tell me.”

John heard a man say to Paty, “Seriously? Randy sent the picture to you.” Paty hung up.

That was fine. John looked at the clock. He was ten minutes late closing up.

He pulled on his windbreaker, snapped off the lights, and stood by the door in the dark for a few moments. He swore, switched the lights on, walked back to the counter, and leaned over to get Vince’s registration form. He took a picture of it with his phone. Then he entered the address on South Polk in Google maps. The image that came up was of a two-story 19th century brick pumping station with a tall tower rising up from the roof. The Black Eye Coffee Shop operated out of the first floor, and the image had captured a bearded hipster sitting at a table outside, sipping an espresso and reading a paperback book.

John entered a search for banks nearby, and the map zoomed out two dozen blocks to the nearest one. Maybe it was a jewelry store or a pawn shop? Not a bank vault, just a vault or a safe. He thought it through. If it was a plan for a heist, it was stupid—break into the pumping station, somehow get to, and then crawl through damaged or crushed old sewage tunnels, and dig into another building through the cement foundation without anyone noticing? He shook his head. Not viable. But a meatball sub was.

A meatball sub shop was around the corner from the pumping station, he might as well get a sub and take a look around. Couldn't hurt.

With his meatball sandwich getting cold in a brown bag on the passenger seat and an RC Cola getting warm in the cup holder, John maneuvered his purple Dodge Dart around a parked flatbed truck and a bulldozer on Water Street. Water Street dead ended at South Polk Street and the old pumping station.

The only problem was the pumping station was gone, torn down. He drove right up to the chain link fence surrounding the hole in the ground. He got out of the car to read the sign—V.B. Construction. It was still plenty light out to see into the big dirt crater. At the bottom of it was the opening to two large tunnels, and they weren't crushed. They looked large enough for a man to crawl into. One ran west and the other went south. The west tunnel led back down Polk Street. Picturing the drawing, the south tunnel, through a series of doglegs, would take water or a person one street over behind the plot to Floyd Street.

John got in his car and backed down Polk for a block and a half to see what was in the squat one-story building next to the empty lot. He stopped at the front door and got out. A sign scribbled in faded marker was pasted to the door. Black Eye Coffee had moved in and then gone out of business. The building was vacant. Back in his car again, John took his meatball sandwich out of the bag. It wasn't a total waste of time.

He was halfway through his dinner when a white Cadillac cruised by. A pretty redhead was at the wheel. As she drove by him, up the street, he read the vanity plate, "Paty362436." She pulled up in front of the empty lot.

The Cadillac idled there for a few minutes. John threw the rest of the sub out of the car window when he saw pink eye walk up to her car. They were too far away for John to hear the conversation, but pink eye's body language read angry.

Out of nowhere, a black SUV flew by and stopped short behind the Cadillac. Two guys with rifles jumped out. John watched stupefied as Paty and pink eye were forced into the back of the SUV. John started his car, hoping they wouldn't drive back the same way and get interested in him and his meatball sub. He couldn't outrun them in his ancient Barney-colored car. The SUV swung around Paty's car and turned down Water Street. John let out the breath he'd been holding and punched 9-1-1 into his phone. He tried to tell the short version of what happened to the operator. She didn't understand the story, but a patrol car was called to the scene.

The police took no time to get there.

John explained to the policeman about the architectural drawings and the bank vault. He filled in more details of the ridiculous story, as he worried that Paty and pink eye were getting buried in some weed field off the interstate.

The cop asked, “License plate on the SUV?”

“I didn’t catch it.”

“The victim’s name is Pinkeye?” the cop asked, not smiling.

“No, he *has* pink eye. His name is Randy.”

“Last name?”

“I don’t know.”

“The other victim is Patty? Last name?”

John shrugged. “This is her car.”

The policeman nodded with diminishing enthusiasm, took notes, and asked when they had been in the library.

John showed the cop the picture of Vince Bauer’s reader registration form with his address and phone number. It also clicked that V.B. Construction probably was Vince’s construction company. The company telephone number was on the sign.

The entire episode was over in a few minutes, and John found himself alone again on the street. He leaned on the hood of his car. He saw what was adjacent to the empty lot, nothing. He wondered what was behind it on Floyd Street.

Back in his car, John drove down Floyd Street and found a hair salon with old fashioned pink hood dryers in the window, a sewing machine repair shop that was out of business, and a florist that specialized, according to the advertising, in funeral arrangements.

John turned his car around. The county building was still open. Night court was in session, and he had better access to answers at work than in his apartment.

When he got there, the security guard was stationed at the front door next to the metal detector. John was going to say hello to him, until he heard his rumbling snores.

John took the steps two at a time to the basement.

The long hallway outside of the library was deserted. He didn’t know what was going to be built on the old pumping station lot. Maybe it was a casino or a hotel. He unlocked the library door and switched on the lights.

He’d been thinking that they were going to go through the old tunnels to get somewhere else, but what if they were planning to use the tunnels to stash something? Money? Drugs?

His cell phone buzzed.

"This is Officer Jessup. The folks are okay. It was some kind of a sex thing."

"What?"

"They paid two guys to pretend to kidnap them and then drop them off at a motel. Nothing illegal there. Maybe not your average date."

"Did you talk to Paty? What about the guns?"

"They didn't file a complaint."

"So, that's it?"

"That's right."

It sure didn't look like a sex thing.

While John had been talking to the officer on the phone, an elderly man in a tweed suit had strolled into the library and stood listening with mild curiosity to John's conversation.

John shoved his phone back in his pocket and asked, "Night court?"

The man nodded.

"It's on the first floor. Take the stairs on the right."

John followed the man to the door, pushed it closed behind him, and locked it.

At his computer, he logged into the library's news subscription database and entered a search. A list of articles about the building project came up. An apartment building was going to be built on the empty lot. It didn't make any sense.

He scanned the list of results, and a headline caught his eye. He opened the article and read that the pumping station had been a block away from where the old restaurant Burl's Steaks and Chops used to be on Floyd Street. John looked up at the water-stained ceiling tiles. He understood it now. He typed in a new search and hit enter.

Someone pounded on the door. John banged his fist on the desk at another interruption and tipped back in his chair. He couldn't see who it was and got up.

Vince and another guy were standing in the hall. John shrank back out of sight when Vince rapped on the glass windowpane in the door with a baseball bat.

John crouched down and scrambled to the other side of the door. The window was bashed in, and shards of glass rained on his head. If he could get to the fire alarm, they would go away. Wet trickles ran down his face as he pulled the fire alarm.

Vince pushed his meaty hand through the shattered glass panel. John grabbed Vince's bandaged, broken finger and yanked it backward. Vince howled and snatched his hand back. The security guard, who was now wide awake, ordered Vince and the other guy to put their hands up.

Two days later, John dropped a brand-new file on the library counter. It contained one item, a news clipping describing how thanks to the city's municipal records librarian and the important records he stewards, the body of a long missing mob informant and owner of Burl's Steaks and Chops House had been found in the south tunnel of the old pumping station. His name was Burl Volpe, and his nickname was Bank Vault.

DINNER AND ...

Bruce Harris

Nola observed the two men from behind an artificial Ficus tree in the hotel lobby. She watched Peter slip three quarters into the vending machine.

"D3," the voice, high-pitched.

Peter turned his head. "Huh?"

"D3," the man repeated. "The Baby Ruth bar. Look at the label. Ten-percent more. Why not get more for your money?" Peter's smile contorted into an oxymoronic amused, annoyed combination. The man noticed. "Let me explain. The candy bar now weighs 9.9 ounces. Obviously, the old, smaller bar was nine ounces. Ten-percent less. The calculation is a simple one. At nine ounces, if the cost is 75-cents, the price per ounce is roughly 8.3 cents. With the added weight, the price drops to slightly more than 7.5 cents per ounce. That's approximately ten-percent less per ounce. See what I'm saying?"

Peter looked at the short, balding man. The stranger's chalky complexion and out of shape sweater gave him a cadaverous appearance. The two were physical opposites. Peter was tall, with a full head of dark, wavy hair. His skin had the appearance of having spent a lot of time under a tropical sun. His clothes, immaculate. Peter's glossy, handmade Italian shoes stood in stark contrast to the stranger's worn chukka boots.

"I don't like nuts," Peter said.

With slightly squinted eyes, the man responded, "Neither do I. Did you know the Baby Ruth bar was named after President Grover Cleveland's eldest daughter, Ruth? Most people think its namesake was Babe Ruth, the baseball player. It wasn't."

"Listen, Mister ..." Peter let the word hang.

"Beebe. Leonard Beebe. I'm here for the annual insurance underwriters conference. I'm an actuary. My tenth year attending. Used to have it downtown, you know, in one of the nicer hotels. No more. Too much money, I guess. Everyone's a bean counter now and cutting back. And you? What brings you here? Family vacation? Business?"

The two men stood in the vending area of the Patriot Hotel in a Philadelphia suburb. Built during the mid-1980's, the hotel was a notch or two above typical airport hotels. Peter had been here before. The place was clean. The staff were professional and accommodating, but best of all, the bar served Stateside, his favorite local small batch vodka.

"Murder." Beebe took an unconscious step back. Peter said nothing, enjoying the awkward silence. Others nearby seemed to pay them no attention, yet they knew better. The two men continued adlibbing.

"Is the victim here, in the hotel?" Beebe questioned.

"Sure is," Peter said, playing along.

"And your motive?" Beebe asked.

"It's not my motive. I'm here to solve the crime, not commit it. This one will be better than last, I hope."

"Oh?" Beebe asked.

"My partner—"

Beebe's grin increased. "So, you have a partner in crime, do you? Who is he?"

Peter didn't hide the annoyance in his voice. "He's a she. Her name's Nola. She's somewhere around." The two men stared at each other. "Okay, I'll tell you," Peter began. "I'm here for a murder mystery dinner party. I met Nola at the last event in Phoenix. We sort of hit it off, if you know what I mean?" Beebe nodded. "We developed a relationship over the past year," Peter said. "We decided to pair up this time, pool our resources, and see if we can't solve this thing together."

"Sounds like fun," Beebe said. "I have to run. Say, you never did tell me your name."

"Peter."

Beebe extended his hand. They shook. "Well, good luck to you and ... what's her name?"

"Nola."

"Right. Nola. Good luck to you both." He turned to leave, but stopped.

"Something wrong?" Peter asked.

"No. Before I leave, I just want to see what candy you finally choose, that's all. One less mystery in this world."

Peter had forgotten about the 75-cents still sitting in the vending machine, awaiting his selection. "I'm glad you reminded me. I might have walked away without anything. Now, that would have been a real crime!" Peter said. "Let's see." He scanned his options. "B4." The plain Hershey chocolate bar fell with a small thud.

"Good choice," Beebe said. "Personally, I would have gone with the Baby Ruth, but given that was the last of the plain Hershey bars, that elevates its value. Nice meeting you, sir. Maybe we'll run into each other again. Who knows?"

Peter watched his acquaintance disappear into the front parking lot. He made his way toward a bowl of apples, but stopped short as his eyes stared up at a wall-mounted monitor. The hotel's daily events displayed. He saw the Red Herring Entertainment's murder mystery dinner listing, but no mention of an insurance convention. He inquired at the front desk. The woman behind the counter wore a HOW CAN I ASSIST? button.

"Is there an insurance company convention at the hotel? I thought there was, but I don't see the listing on your daily activities screen."

She punched a keyboard, scanned a screen, and shook her head. "No, I don't see anything." She held up a pale-pink painted nail. "One moment." She asked a colleague, but returned shaking her head. "No, I'm sorry. Perhaps I can help you locate it? Maybe it's in another hotel nearby?"

"No, never mind," Peter said. He hoped his demeanor didn't convey annoyance. He punched the elevator for the fourth floor. Thoughts of Nola replaced Leonard Beebe.

Nola had been watching the entire time. She waited 30-minutes before using the key Peter had given her and let herself in. She saw Peter sprawled out on the bed, unmoving. The empty candy wrapper lay crumbled on the end table. Before waving Leonard Beebe inside, Nola took a piece of the wrapper and pocketed it. Beebe poked his head in, then strode forward with cockiness.

"I told you it'd be easy," he said. Beebe moved to embrace Nola, but she pushed him away.

"Not now. There's plenty of time for that. Let's get what we came for and get the hell out of here."

Beebe backed off. He took Peter's wallet, removed the cash, and tossed the alligator-skin to the floor. He removed Peter's Patek Phillipe watch and strapped it to his own wrist.

"Damn, that's one sweet-looking honey of a timepiece," he said. "Has a nice heft to it."

"Don't get used to it. Give me the cash," Nola ordered.

Without taking his eyes off the watch, Beebe handed her the money. He glanced back at Peter. "Poor sonofabitch. He had the poor misfortune of being wealthy and falling for the likes of you," he said. He practically salivated while looking into Nola's eyes. "Can't say I blame him, though."

"Aren't you forgetting something?" Nola asked.

"What?"

"The wrapper. Or, are you planning to leave it there for the police?"

Beebe whistled. "Ha! That would be something, wouldn't it? After all this planning? Brains and beauty. That's what I like about you. Me? I'm just a delivery man filling vending machines with sweets and overly salted snacks. But, no one knows how to place an aconite-laced Hershey bar in such a strategic location as Leonard Beebe." He thumped his chest.

"I told you our deceased friend hated nuts and wouldn't select anything with nuts."

"That's why I stocked the machine with nuts-only candy ... with one exception, that is." There was no humor in his laughter. "Okay, I'll lay low for a while, like we agreed. Just make sure you keep the DO NOT DISTURB sign on the door."

"Don't worry about my end of things," Nola said. "Our dead friend here won't be discovered for another two days. Now, take off the watch and give it to me until everything blows over. Like we agreed," she added, mimicking Beebe.

The vending machine route man reluctantly handed Nola the wristwatch, grabbed what remained of the wrapper from the table and stuffed it into his pocket. "I'll get rid of the evidence," he said and walked out.

And I'll get rid of you, Nola thought, *like I did Peter and the two before him.* Once Beebe was gone, she placed the piece of candy wrapper she had taken earlier back onto the table. She scribbled a note to the police. She'd call them and report Beebe, the poisoned chocolate, and the body. But first, she planned to eat dinner and partake in a murder mystery.

A talented musician, Nola took to the violin as a child. Her parents were successful in everything, except parenting. Both facts evident as she performed *Funeral March of a Marionette*, her bare legs spread ever so slightly but enough to make Fred Taylor squirm in his seat. She had the instrument and the man where she wanted them. It was a nice warmup to both the dinner-murder mystery crowd and Fred Taylor, a successful hedge fund manager. He had no real interest in the night's performance, but it was as good an excuse to shack up with Nola as any.

Nola finished, bowed to the applauding audience, and rushed over to Taylor's table. Alongside Taylor were dinner theater regulars John and Debbie McKinley. Nola gave Taylor a cheek kiss. He held out her chair. She placed the encased violin on the floor and sat down.

"So, what did you think?" she asked with a coy, fleeting glance in Taylor's direction.

“Loved it. The theme to the old Alfred Hitchcock Presents show. Great little song,” Debbie said.

“We still watch weeknights when we can’t sleep,” John added. Despite having attended numerous such dinners, he felt the staged cloak and dagger plays childish and boorish. He acquiesced to appease Debbie. She was one of Red Herring Entertainment’s many rabid fans. Several of the “regulars” competed against each other.

“Marvelous. Enticing,” Taylor said, his eyes scanning her legs. “And, by the sound of the applause, everyone felt the same way. Put us all in the mood for murder,” he said. The table’s occupants chuckled.

Taylor offered Nola the celery bowl. She grabbed a stalk, dipped it into a saucer of blue-cheese dressing and took a seductive bite. A precocious child, Nola learned long ago how to use her charms to get what she wanted. She grew up in a wealthy, although dysfunctional home. Her father rose with meteoric speed to become the senior buyer for a nationwide hardware store chain. His frequent travel schedule made him mostly unavailable to Nola and her mother. Not the warmest soul, Nola’s father divided people into leaders and followers. There was no in between. The only useful purpose followers served was enhancing leaders’ lives. Nola discovered at an early age the meaning of Machiavellianism. Nola, an only-child, and her mother responded differently to their environment. Her mother numbed herself with alcohol while abdicating all motherly functions, choosing instead to pay a revolving door of nannies to care for Nola. Music filled a void in young Nola’s life. She became as proficient with a bow and violin in her hands as she had controlling men, especially wealthy men. Fred Taylor was only the latest. Her most recent, a money manager of some sort named Peter, had been her latest victim. There were other victims as well. Nola had long ago become skilled at the old badger con game, but Peter was the first she’d murdered. Actually, she just called the shots. Some loser, or follower as her father would have classified him, named Beebe did the deed and would take the fall. Beebe filled vending machines. He planted an aconite-laced chocolate bar in the hotel lobby vending machine. Through careful planning, it was arranged that Peter would select the tainted bar and ingest it. Things had gone according to plan. Nola thought about Peter’s body in the 4th floor hotel room. She had not gotten around to contacting the police yet. There was no rush. She was certain the smitten Beebe wouldn’t be going anywhere.

“These are the McKinleys,” Taylor’s voice said, introducing John and Debbie.

“Like the president,” John McKinley said.

“He was assassinated, you know?” Debbie added. “Shot.”

As if she knew them for years, a warm smile emerged on Nola's face. "So nice to meet you both," she said. "Shot, you say? Well, that's certainly appropriate for a murder mystery night." She turned toward Taylor. "Are we sure the McKinleys are not part of tonight's ensemble?"

Taylor scratched his chin. "Hmm, now that you mention it—"

"Oh, heavens no!" interrupted Debbie. "We're contestants, just like yourselves." After a brief pause, "You are contestants, aren't you?" she asked.

"We'll never tell," a winking Taylor said.

The foursome continued making small talk throughout the dinner. John couldn't help but notice Taylor's clothes and jewelry. The man had bucks, that was clear. McKinley wished to himself that he had that kind of FU money.

The food was not particularly good, it never was at these productions. But, people didn't pay for the food, rather, the night's entertainment and the challenge of solving a carefully plotted fictional murder mystery. Tension mounted while dessert and coffee were served. No murder or crime had yet occurred. Nola pulled away the pudding dish in front of Taylor.

"Hey, what are you doing?" he asked.

"Oh please," Nola said, summoning up her most pitiful voice. "I do so love banana pudding, and I rejected the dessert option when we registered. Please, be a doll and give me your portion. I'll make it worth your while." Her smile spoke volumes.

"Well, I don't know—"

Nola pulled a chocolate Hershey bar from her handbag. "Here, have this instead. You like chocolate, don't you?"

"Well ... yes ... but—"

"Then it's a deal," Nola said with authority. She began giggling.

"What's so funny?" Taylor asked.

The comment surprised Nola. She hadn't realized her laughter was audible. "Save it for later. Don't eat it now," she said, leaning into Taylor's ear. "I have special plans for you and that chocolate bar."

Taylor sat back in his chair, his thoughts not ones typically conjured up Sunday mornings. This time, Nola made sure her laughter remained within. Poor Peter lay dead four floors above, courtesy of a poisonous chocolate bar. Taylor was next on Nola's hit parade. She already had her eyes on his massive gold watch and heavy, diamond ring.

Most in the room had finished desserts and were on their second or third cups of coffee, when one of the servers collapsed.

"Oh my God! Ralph, are you okay? Ralph? Is there a doctor in the house?" shouted another server.

"I'm a doctor," came a voice from the front of the room. A man in a three-piece suit rushed to the fallen employee. "It must be fate," he declared. "I was on my way to use the restroom when I heard a call for a doctor."

"Wow, what a break!" shouted one of the chefs. "How is he, doc?"

"He's dead." declared the doctor.

"Just a moment." A man and woman stood up from a rear table. The taller of the two, the woman, said, "Nobody leaves this room, and that includes you, Doctor. I'm Detective Rawlings and this is Detective Schulman. We're in charge for now."

A giddy Debbie McKinley elbowed her husband. "This is it!" she said. "This is what we came for. I hope you've been paying attention, John. There are clues everywhere."

John grinned, nodded. *Here we go again*, he thought. *I don't know why she thinks these far-fetched crimes are fun.*

Fred Taylor played along but he also wasn't amused. His thoughts were on Nola and what the two of them would be doing once this farce of a skit was over.

The two detectives divided up the room and began questioning the guests. After half an hour, Rawlings and Schulman huddled. They emerged and walked toward the Nola, Taylor, and McKinley table. Rawlings took charge.

"You four," she began, "stand up and walk over to the body, please."

The table's occupants complied. Debbie McKinley practically leaped from her chair to follow Rawlings. "Oh well, looks like you caught us," Debbie joked. She slowed her pace near table seven, then stopped for a quick chat with two women. John recognized them as Helen Stone and her mother, Lenore. Helen was Debbie's not-so-friendly competitor at these mystery dinners. John couldn't have cared less who solved the insipid crimes, but it irked Debbie every time Helen solved it and took home some worthless prize or certificate. Fact was, more often than not, Helen won. Inevitably, during the ride home, John was subjected to Debbie's diatribes about how she thought Helen cheated, or bribed one of the actors. Debbie refused to accept the notion that Helen consistently outsmarted her fair and square. John secretly enjoyed the tension between the two. He simply couldn't believe how anyone could get worked up over such trivial nonsense. After a few words, Debbie, appearing smug as ever, walked away from Helen's table and joined Rawlings and Schulman in the room's center.

While the foursome and Rawlings huddled around the acting dead man, Detective Schulman examined the table. He saw the Hershey bar next to Taylor's napkin. He took it, unwrapped it, and walked toward Nola and the others. He took a bite.

Nola felt Schulman's presence and turned toward him. Momentarily frozen, she regained her composure, ripping the candy from Schulman's hand. "Stop! Where did you get that?"

"From the tab—"

"Spit it out! Quickly! Spit it out!" she yelled.

Debbie McKinley's eyes widened. "Ha! I knew it. John, I told you these two were part of the play. This is so exciting."

Rawlings and Schulman stared at each other. Ralph, the actor playing dead on the floor, opened his eyes. "What the hell's going on?" Taylor asked. "Nola, you're in on this? Really?"

No one noticed the two men who had entered the dining hall. They approached the group in the room's center, showing badges. There was nothing phony about them. Nola recognized the two as Peter and Leonard Beebe. Blood drained from her face. "You? What? How ..." but the words hung in the air. Peter grabbed hold of Nola's elbow.

"I assure you there's nothing wrong with the chocolate," Peter said to Schulman. "I've eaten a similar one. Caloric, but delicious." He turned toward Taylor. "Nola is in on the murder, but not this one."

"Attempted murder," Beebe chimed in. "Among other charges."

"You two set me up?" Nola sneered. Her reddened face distorted.

The two real detectives, Peter and Beebe began escorting Nola out of the room. A numb Taylor trailed behind. Peter stopped, excused himself, and turned around. He walked back toward the huddled group.

"Our case is finished," Peter said to the McKinleys, "but it appears," his gaze shifted toward the prostrate Ralph, "as though yours is just beginning." He knelt down inches from Ralph's ear. "Here's some advice from someone with experience. Keep your eyes closed when you're playing dead."

FACE THE MUSIC

A You-Solve-It By Peter DiChellis

Storm clouds rumbled across the noon sky as Detective Lissetta Muldoon and her young partner Detective Benito Dalpaz arrived at the murder scene, the luxury condominium apartment and home office of independent music producer Nicky Grannin.

"Poisoned," the Medical Examiner said. "Fast-acting poison in his coffee. Dead within seconds."

Muldoon scrutinized the scene. Grannin was slumped over his home-office desk, the fingers of his right hand clutching the handle of a royal blue coffee cup in a gruesome death grip. He wore a gaudy red Hawaiian shirt. A green dragon tattoo emblazoned his left forearm. Across from him, a second coffee cup lingered on the desk. A smear of lipstick on the brim faced the visitor's chair. The handles of both cups pointed toward a bookcase teeming with music industry awards.

"Nicky Grannin had a sharp ear for talent," Dalpaz said. "Turned unknown club musicians into recording stars." The young detective gave a sad shake of his head. "A shame he never heard my garage band."

The building's security camera system wasn't working and the doorman had called in sick that day, so Muldoon examined Grannin's phone. The Calendar app showed no meetings but the Notes section referenced two for that morning. The jumbled notes included names, phone numbers, and abbreviated background info, but no meeting times. Muldoon concluded Grannin was either secretive about his business affairs or simply disorganized. She found only one recent call, incoming, which had gone to voicemail: "Hey Mr. Grannin, it's Roy the one-handed ukulele player again. Seems like I call every week. Hope you'll catch my show at the carnival tonight. I'll leave your name at the door. Or call me and I'll drop by this morning with free tickets."

Muldoon called back and left a voicemail. She didn't mention Grannin was dead. "This guy's probably not the killer, but we need to talk to him," she told Dalpaz.

Dalpaz scheduled interviews with the two people Grannin noted he'd meet that morning, a country-western songwriter known as Crystal Creeks and a punk rocker with the stage name Fiona Trashcan. Dalpaz didn't tell them Grannin was dead.

The detectives met Fiona at the coffee shop where she worked her day job. She stood behind the service counter, elaborate tattoos covering her neck, iridescent pink streaks highlighting her dark hair. Her left arm was enclosed in a cast from elbow to fingertips. She was not wearing lipstick.

"What happened to your arm?" Dalpaz blurted out.

"Broken. I fell off the stage last Saturday night after just the right amount of tequila. Didn't feel a thing."

Muldoon intervened. "You're a potential witness to a crime not a suspect," she lied. "You can stop the interview any time. But before we start, I need you to sign a statement saying you understand your rights."

"What crime?" Fiona asked, but Muldoon simply placed the statement on the counter for a signature. Fiona shrugged and signed it with stylish cursive penmanship.

Muldoon began the interview.

"I met Nicky Grannin this morning, just after ten o'clock," Fiona said. "I went totally prepared, wore stage makeup and everything, so he could see my brand persona. He's a tough audience. I begged him to produce my album, working title: 'Violent Ball of Garbage.' My music exposes the world's moral corruption. It's my gift."

The detectives finished the interview and moved on to meet country-western songwriter Crystal Creeks at her apartment.

Crystal greeted the detectives in red sweatpants, a faded orange t-shirt, and a platinum blonde hairstyle that added five inches to her height. She was not wearing lipstick. Country music posters decorated her apartment walls and a guitar lay in an open case on the tattered carpet.

"You play guitar. Same as me." The young Dalpaz pointed to the open case. "But your strings look wrong."

"It's strung upside down," Crystal said. "Left-handed."

"You're a potential witness to a crime not a suspect," Muldoon lied again. "You can stop the interview any time. But before we start, I need you to sign a statement saying you understand your rights."

"What happened?" Crystal asked, but Muldoon simply handed her the statement for her signature. Crystal signed it with a flourish and the detectives began the interview.

"I met Nicky Grannin this morning, shortly after ten o'clock," Crystal said. "Got all dolled up for it: sequined denims, buckskin blazer, full makeup. I begged him to produce my new song. He's a tough audience." She began singing in a nasal voice with a country twang: '*On our ten-year anniversary my husband stole my truck and left. It broke my heart, broke my heart, because I loved to drive that truck.*'" Crystal beamed. "There's more, but you get the idea."

Muldoon's phone buzzed. A callback from Roy, the one-handed ukulele player at the carnival.

"I guess you called about Nicky Grannin," he said. "I know what happened. I heard it from a freak who works in the sideshow here. He heard it from his ex-wife, who's in the funeral business. I'm sorry Mr. Grannin is dead. A shame he never heard me play one-handed ukulele."

Muldoon spoke a few words into the phone, ended the call, and pulled Dalpaz aside. "I know who killed Nicky Grannin," she told him. "Let's make an arrest."

"Ready when you are," Dalpaz said.

Four hours later, beneath blinding lights in a grimy interrogation room, Muldoon's suspect broke down and confessed.

How'd you solve it?" Dalpaz asked afterward.

Solution in next month's issue ...

SOLUTION TO MAY'S YOU-SOLVE-IT

Ants, Plants And Romance By Jeffrey A. Lockwood

Sheriff Jenkins pulled out a pair of handcuffs and snapped them onto Mr. Gordon's inflamed wrists, much to the outrage of Miss Sturgeon, along with the thief who threatened to have his lawyer empty the coffers of Teton County when he sued for false arrest.

"Slow down pardners," said Jenkins, "and let this backwoods lawman explain."

Miss Sturgeon grabbed her cell phone and said, "You had better be quick, or I'll make a call that will end your pathetic career."

"Now then, there's no cause for insults and threats little lady," said Jenkins, laying a Western drawl on thick to aggravate both victim and perpetrator. It was his job to apprehend the latter, but that didn't mean he had to kowtow to the former. Although the sheriff wasn't much concerned about his job, some of the county commissioners were tight with outside millionaires.

"I demand to call my attorney," said Mr. Gordon.

"Hold your horses. First I need to save my pathetic career in law enforcement from Miss Sturgeon's wrath. As I figure it ma'am, this fellow was ogling not only your ample cleavage but your diamond necklace at dinner last night." She began to object, but he held up a hand and continued. "His plan to divest you from your virtue unfolded that evening and his plan to separate you from your diamonds unfolded the next morning, starting with detaching the television cable. An experienced jewel thief would figure that a maintenance man is an ideal fall guy, while a 'country bumpkin' maid, as you put it Miss Sturgeon, would make a weak suspect for hotel security to pursue."

"But Parker was with me all day, except for his short nap in the afternoon. And he didn't have a key to my cabin."

"I didn't quite know how he'd pulled off the heist until I saw that rash on his arms. You won't find poison ivy in the Tetons, but the wall surrounding the hot tub out back is covered in clematis. Its sap is very irritating as my mother reminds me when I get to trimming her yard. So, it seems that Mr. Gordon didn't need a nap as much as he wanted a necklace. He lied to you about the glass door being locked in the morning, so he climbed the wall entangling himself in the vines, then slid open the door and nabbed the necklace. To cover his tracks, your sweetie locked the back door and left out the front door which locked behind him."

"That's a fine story, but your only evidence is a rash which could've come from anywhere. Obviously, the maid or maintenance man took the necklace in the morning," Mr. Gordon said with a tone of self-satisfaction.

"Except for two things," said Jenkins. "I know that the door was opened after the resort staff left in the morning. When you came into the cabin, a few winged ants joined you. My six-legged informants emerge for mating following rain and there was a storm in the afternoon. That's just another little bit of outdoors knowledge that comes from living in the boondocks."

"You said two things, Sheriff," said Miss Sturgeon now looking fondly at the grizzled lawman.

"Yes'm. While you two were at dinner tonight, my deputy wandered into Mr. Gordon's cabin and found a diamond necklace."

"You need a warrant to search a person's accommodations. My lawyer will have that evidence thrown out so fast it'll make your head spin," Mr. Gordon sneered. "And without the necklace, you have nothing more than folksy speculation."

"You're right, pardner. But in these parts, the sheriff and a district court judge might just be old high school buddies. And a judge might owe the sheriff a favor for looking past a misguided, teenaged nephew having a little Colorado pot in his pickup. And so a search warrant based on folksy speculation might be issued faster than a rattlesnake strikes. And a thief's fancy lawyer might just aggravate a backwater judge so that the accused gets sentenced a little harsher than if he'd learned some manners and respect. So my advice is for you to exercise your right to remain silent. And you, Miss Sturgeon, might think about a very generous tip for the maid as an apology for assuming our local girls have no more principles than yourself."

www.ingramcontent.com/pod-product-compliance
Ingram Content Group UK Ltd.
Pitfield, Milton Keynes, MK11 3LW, UK
UKHW061701190726
13853UKWH00008B/2336

9 798510 789768